THE
SECRET
GRAVE

THE SECRET GRAVE

HAUNTINGS

LOIS RUBY

SCHOLASTIC INC.

ISBN 978-0-545-93250-9

10 9 8 7 6 5 4 3   17 18 19 20 21

Printed in the U.S.A.   40

First printing 2017

Book design by Christopher Stengel

FOR THE CHILDREN, TEACHERS, AND LIBRARIANS
IN GEORGIA WHO HAVE MADE THE
PEACH STATE MY SECOND HOME

CHAPTER ONE

LOTS OF PEOPLE DON'T REALIZE THAT SOME nightshade plants are poisonous. I mean, deadly poisonous. But that has nothing to do with why our house is called Nightshade. Autumn Splendor is its real name. Could there possibly be a more boring name for a fabulous old mansion that's been sprawling here on Thornbury Trace for a hundred and twenty years? The house is three stories tall with fourteen rooms and one of those wraparound porches just made for stargazing and sipping lemonade. The house went on the market last year, and my sweet, sentimental dad snapped it up because his grandparents had lived in Autumn Splendor a long time ago, just after World War II, but they only stayed about a year. I wonder why. Well, I wonder *why* a lot of things.

We moved in last winter when it was cold enough for the water leaking from most of the faucets to freeze midstream. People up north think it's always hot here in Georgia, but they're wrong. It can get deadly cold. The house creaked and groaned, and some stairs dipped from the pounding of millions of footsteps. When you least expected it, the hardwood floors slanted east. The wind rattled windows, and don't get me started on the drafts that crept in under doors that refused to shut tight. No wonder it was vacant for six months!

"It's a delightfully quirky house," Mom said that first day as she flipped on the light switch and blew a circuit that plunged all seven of us into darkness.

Gracie, who's almost three, wailed and buried her head in Mom's sweatshirt.

"It's a nightmare. All these shadows make me crazy," my older sister Franny grumbled. Grumbling is her most cheerful way of talking.

The boys, Scooter and Trick, huddled with me on the steps as if we were waiting for the morning sunrise at three in the afternoon.

"Hey, Hannah, don't you think it would be cool if the electricity never came back on?" Scooter asked me. He was already sneezing and wheezing because of all the dust that had settled in a house empty for months and months. *What if we can't get Scooter's humidifier or breathing machine going?* I wondered. I'm the big worrier in the family.

Trick reminded us, "No lights, no TV, no WiFi, no microwave, no hot pizza. Doomsday."

Franny groaned piteously. "I'm getting a twelve-aspirin headache."

"Not me. I'm getting a brilliant idea!" Dad said, feeling his way to the breaker box under the stairs. "Ages ago, when my grandparents bought this house, the owners said it was called Nightshade. My grandma didn't like the name and went back to Autumn Splendor, the original name. That's fine for a stodgy, ordinary place. But this house is spectacular. It's dark and mysterious, and now that it's ours, I move that we go back to the perfect name for our shadowy house. Nightshade."

"Second the motion!" we all cried, except Franny, of course. Now that the lights were back on, we started hauling personal treasures and sports equipment and Gracie's toys and groceries into the house before the two moving vans arrived with our furniture.

It's weird that we call the house by name like it's the eighth member of our family. Say we're heading home from a day at the county fair, all cotton-candy sticky, and Gracie's asleep on Dad's shoulder. He'll say, "Well, kiddos, let's hotfoot it back to Nightshade."

An old house with a name that cool and creepy has to have ghosts, right? I'm always listening for creaky footsteps in the dark and doors slamming in empty rooms and water gurgling through the pipes when everyone else is asleep. Ghostly signs. Not that I believe in ghosts.

But if the real thing doesn't turn up, all eerie and spooky and Halloweenish, why don't I just appoint myself, me, Hannah Eileen Flynn, the official Ghost of Nightshade?

One of the best things about our house is its huge attic, and the only way to get to the attic is by pulling down a ladder in my bedroom. Did I choose the right room, or what? Next to my room is Dad's studio, with a balcony that seems to just hang off the edge of the house. We don't dare step foot on that balcony until Dad can get a carpenter out here to check it out and make sure we won't fall to our deaths. We couldn't even if we wanted to, anyway, because the door is painted shut, which raises lots of questions.

A bunch of the house's front windows, like big eager eyes, look out over grass and shrubs and nothing else for a half a mile on either side of us. Best of all, Nightshade backs up to a forest. Big old houses with woods for backyards have got to harbor ghosts, and ghosts probably hibernate in the winter, like bears and bats. But now that it's June and school is out, I'm dying to know what surprises the woods and Nightshade have in store for us this summer.

Something eerie and shivery, I hope.

CHAPTER TWO

"HANNAH FLYNN, YOU ARE THE ONLY PERSON whose birthday cake is a raspberry pie," Luisa says, while Mom yanks twelve candles and the good-luck one out of a warm pie the size of a truck's hubcap. It's a jumbo pie because my family is huge, but Dad's taken my siblings to McDonald's so I can have a peaceful birthday with my two best friends. I'm the only one in the Flynn zoo who craves quiet and order. Sometimes I think I was switched at birth with an alien bot-baby.

Probably not. I do have an actual human mother, who looks just like me and who writes an advice column called "Dear Bettina." Her column is syndicated in hundreds of small-town newspapers under a glamorous picture of her. If only her readers could see her now, in her baggy red sweats with GO GEORGIA BULLDOGS down the leg stripe. She plops a scoop of ice cream on each of our plates. Choco-late melting and drizzling down the sides of the warm pie, yum! When I die and get to heaven, I'm ordering hot raspberry pie with chocolate ice cream for dessert every day. Wait, do you get a menu in heaven?

A mouthful of pie mooshes Sara's words: "Don't forget, next month's *my* birthday."

Like we could forget, since she reminds us twenty times a day. Luisa and Sara and I have been friends forever, but Sara can't get over the fact that I turn a year older before she does.

Mom smiles at Sara, who says, "I promise y'all a real birthday cake, gooey yellow roses, curlicue writing, the whole beautiful mess."

"And tomorrow I leave for Woodmont," Luisa says. She's crazy-excited about winning a camp scholarship from the Shriners. "Wish you two were coming with me. Three awesome weeks with all those new friends I haven't met yet. Well, just summer friends," she adds quickly. "Y'all are my real friends."

"Luck-*ee*," Sara moans, scraping up every bit of pie on her plate. "I'm out of here Saturday, too, but it's just to my grandma's in Iowa. Iowa is so Midwest."

My brother Trick would give his right eyeball to go to that Kevin Costner *Field of Dreams* place in Iowa where they built a baseball diamond out in the middle of a cornfield.

Sara's still talking. "I'll be swimming in a stinky pond with my bratty cousins until I'm a prune. And there'll be corn, corn, corn wherever you look."

"Don't forget that boy Joey you met last summer," Luisa reminds her.

"If he totally ignores me like he did last year, I've still got London to look forward to after Iowa. Me, at Buckingham Palace with Kate and William and their two adorable prince and princess kids!"

Luisa says, "It's not like they're going to invite you in for pizza, if the royal cooks even know how to make a deep-dish pepperoni. Best you'll get from the royal family is a wave from the balcony."

"I hope I see Kate up close. Her hair is so gorgeous," Sara adds.

"William's kind of cute, too, even if he's practically bald."

They're so psyched about their summer plans that they don't even notice me shriveling into my own freckly skin while ice cream melts into a bloody-looking puddle on my plate.

This summer I'm going exactly nowhere.

Sara thrusts a gift bag toward me. "Open it!"

I know what it is. Luisa and Sara always give me T-shirts with wacky messages, and then they borrow them back, and they look way better in them than I do.

They're both tall and limby, and I'm short and stumpy, without much neck to brag about. A turtleneck reaches past my chin to my lower lip. Adorable.

"Oh, good one!" I chirp. The black shirt says WELL-BEHAVED WOMEN SELDOM MAKE HISTORY. I slip it on over my tank top.

"The minute we saw it on Facebook, Luisa and I knew it was *you*, since you're already historically famous at school for being the first one to smell the kitchen fire."

Big deal. Well, the disaster in our cafeteria *did* make the front page of the Dalton *Daily Citizen*, but I toss off the compliment with fake humility. "You can't miss the aroma of three hundred burning grilled cheese sandwiches."

"Ewww! I will never eat a grilled cheese again. We'll probably have 'em, like, three times a week at camp."

"Nobody in London would be caught dead eating grilled cheese," Sara boasts.

I jump up to get the milk so she won't see me roll my eyes. Three gallon jugs fight one another for space on the top shelf of the fridge, since all five of us kids are guzzlers.

Sara carries her smeared plate to the sink. "Thanks for the pie, Mrs. Flynn. I gotta go home to do some laundry for my trip. I'm going to London, or did I mention that already?" she asks with a crinkly grin.

Luisa's chair squeaks as she stands up. "I'm outta here, too."

Of course. If Sara goes, Luisa follows. Sometimes I feel like the third wheel on a bike.

"Happy birthday, Hannah. I'll text you later," Luisa promises. The kitchen screen door slams behind them, and I still haven't taken a bite of my pie. I will shrivel up like an overripe peach before they come back. It's going to be a hot, lonely, boring summer.

CHAPTER THREE

Before the whole family bombards our kitchen and digs into the raspberry pie, I slip away to the peaceful forest behind our house. We aren't supposed to wander past the first row of pine trees. This spring a tree fell across the path when it was struck by lightning. I guess that's nature's way of saying KIDS, KEEP OUT! It doesn't apply to me, of course. *Well-behaved women seldom make history.* I swing my legs over the giant log, and my sneakers squish a bed of leaves that's decaying after yesterday's typical Georgia summer downpour.

It's that part of the early evening when everything looks gray and hazy and your eyes deceive you. I wander deeper into the woods over a narrow path that someone has tamped down. I never noticed that before, and who could have done it, since nobody ever comes here but my brother Scooter and me? Through a clearing I see the fading sun glint off Moonlight Lake, which Scooter calls Pukey Pond. Dad has warned us a zillion times to stay away from it. He says it's surrounded by sinkholes and snakes, those disgusting creatures whose only claim to fame is that they swallow mice whole. Snakes are not my favorite animals. People are. My favorite animals, I mean.

The last slice of sun is setting into the water in circles of blue and pink light. Suddenly the sun drops to the depths of the lake, and the forest is darker — too dark to spot a treacherous sinkhole, much less a lurking snake. A shiver squiggles up my spine and prickles my ears. I glance over my shoulder to see if I'd be able to sprint out of the woods if I got bitten, before the venom could stampede through my body.

Nothing behind me looks familiar. It's as though the trees have clumped together to block my path. My skin begins to crawl, and my heart thumps a loud drumbeat in this silent forest. I feel totally alone, and though I'm usually the one who craves alone time, right now it feels menacing.

I don't dare walk forward, but I can't see my way out of the woods, either. My feet move on their own as my eyes dart from tree to tree. Two, three, four more steps back. Where am I? What if I never find my way out? I could end up a skinless bundle of sunburnt bones, all the rest of me munched up by opossums and raccoons. Are raccoons carnivores? Deer aren't, but there aren't any Bambis in this forest, are there? No bears, right?

I keep backing up, hoping my feet will automatically retrace their steps — and I nearly land in the lap of a girl perched on a stone bench! I'm sure I've never seen that bench in all the times I've wandered in the woods.

"You scared me to death!"

She chuckles. "I'm glad to see you're still kicking." Her voice is as thin as ribbon, and she's not at all surprised to see me.

"Who are you?" I demand.

Faded blue eyes stare into mine until I look away. "My name is Cady."

"Cady who?"

"Just Cady. That's who I am," she says as if she wishes she were somebody else.

"How did you get here without me hearing or seeing you?"

Her warm smile promises no answer. Brown hair twisted into a loose knot at the top of her head is held in place with two sticks that look like tree twigs. Wispy curls frame her face, coiled at her pasty-looking cheeks. This girl needs some sunshine! The collar of her long flowery dress is tight around her swan neck. Pointed sleeves nearly cover small hands with half-moon fingernails. She's got to be sweating like a pig in all those clothes.

"Did you just move into the neighborhood?" I ask, even though there aren't any houses for half a mile.

"No, I've been here a long time," she says.

"I know everybody in Dalton. Everybody my age." Wouldn't I have noticed a girl dressed like she's from another century? I mean, that kind of getup stands out at school. "I don't remember seeing you at Brookwood or Dalton Middle."

"Maybe you weren't looking in the right places."

What an annoying answer. And it makes me even more suspicious. "What do your parents do?"

"Do you always treat new friends like they're criminals?"

I step back, stung by her comment. I guess I have been interrogating her. "I'm a nosy person."

"I know." Those faded eyes sharpen again, drilling into my own. "You're Hannah-in-the-Middle, right? I'm so happy to meet you, finally. I've been waiting for you."

"Waiting for me? What do you mean? And how do you know what my family calls me?"

"Your family's noisy. Voices carry."

"All this distance?"

"If you're a good listener." Cady pats the bench beside her. It looks inviting, the stone cool and curved to fit my rear. "We know some of the same people."

"At school?"

"Yeah, there. I see you around. I'm very observant. It's easy when you're on your own."

She says it so sadly that I make a snap decision to squeeze her in at our lunch table the first day back to school. Luisa and Sara and the others will just have to get used to her. Maybe I can give her some gentle pointers on what to wear. I glance down at my T-shirt and faded cut-offs. I'm not exactly a fashion queen, but at least my clothes don't look like I inherited them from my grandmother.

Something rustles behind me. "What's that?" I turn, hoping it's just a tree frog or a night loon. Whatever it is, it's quiet now, as if it knows I'm hunting for it. When I turn back, Cady is gone! Did I offend her with too many questions?

And now it's as if the trees have parted like curtains on a stage, and I can clearly see my way out of the woods. I feel like *Alice in Wonderland*, or maybe *Ella, Enchanted*. Someone trapped in a world where nothing makes sense. Am I imagining a girl called Cady who comes and goes on silent feet?

CHAPTER FOUR

A DASH THROUGH THE TALL PINES GETS ME TO THE felled log at the mouth of the forest. Relief washes through me when I swing my legs over the log to the safe side and the flickering lights of my house welcome me. Everyone should be home by now, wondering where I am. I've got to get Scooter alone. He's the only one I can tell what I saw in the woods.

If it actually happened — Cady, the bench, our strange conversation. It was so real and yet so unbelievable, as if a bright light switched on in the night in the woods, which reminds me of a poem we had to memorize in English class last semester:

"Tyger Tyger, burning bright, in the forests of the night."

I guess the dead white guy who wrote that poem didn't know how to spell tiger. Breathless, I open the screen door.

Mom's alone in the kitchen, unloading the dishwasher to make room for our pie plates. "Where have you been for the last hour, Hannah?"

"It's my birthday. Can't I go for a walk without being interrogated like a criminal?" Doesn't *that* sound familiar! And a tad too snappish, so I grab up a few plates to put in the cupboard. Best way to distract a parent — offer to help.

Mom backs off. "Sure, baby. Newly minted twelve-year-olds are entitled to disappear for a while. Uh-oh, brace yourself, here comes the gang."

The boys burst through the door. Patrick, alias Trick, is fourteen and has his phone blasting the Atlanta Braves game. Baseball is his life, though our older sister Franny says he couldn't hit a ball with a bat the size of a tree trunk.

"Yo," he says, ear pressed to his phone.

"Turn it down, Trick." Mom tells him that every time he walks into a room during baseball season.

"Ooh, yeah, pie!" Scooter yelps, licking his lips gecko-like. Scooter's amazing. He has a really tough time with asthma and we never know when he's going to be hit with an attack. The doctor says he'll outgrow it eventually, but while he's waiting for that to happen, he never complains. We all try not to fuss over him, which is why Trick now holds Scooter off with a fork aimed at his heart.

"Me first, I'm older," Trick says. Raspberry goo oozes out as he digs his fork into the uncut part of the pie.

"Patrick, manners!" Mom yells. "And turn that phone down a decibel or two."

I send a message toward Scooter in pantomime and eye flares: *need to talk to you*. He nods. Message received. He's a year younger than I am, and my favorite in the family, although we're not supposed to have favorites.

Franny swirls into the kitchen with Gracie on her hip. "Ugh, that awful bloody-looking pie again?"

Mom says, "Be nice, Frances, it's your sister's birthday."

"Just sayin'." Franny is seventeen, so everything annoys her. Gracie hangs off Franny's left arm, stretching her grubby index finger dangerously close to the pie.

"Don't you dare, baby," Mom warns, offering her the dripping chocolate ice cream scoop, which she licks like a lollipop. Then Gracie crawls under the table where she'll probably untie everyone's shoelaces. Her idea of a giggle riot.

Last in is Dad, who tosses his car keys on the counter. He won't be able to find them tomorrow because the counter is cluttered with sticky juice glasses and sippy cups, a ripped Cheerios box, guppy food, two avocado plants, and Trick's mitt. If I had to describe our house in one word, it would be *stuffed*.

Dad beams at us, his lips wide and pink between his mustache and his beard. He's Mr. Major Family Man, happy with all the chaos of a tribe of kids, from seventeen to two. Which sounds like the score of one of Trick's baseball games.

When Franny's in a good mood, she calls me Hannah-in-the-Middle, like Jack-in-the-Box, which I hate. (And how did Cady actually *hear* that?)

"Do you feel like the middle button?" Franny once asked me, and I knew just what she meant. I'm the middle button on the back of a sundress that you can't quite reach from the top down, or from the waist up. I couldn't see the back of that awful dress Cady was wearing, but I'll bet it had about fifteen buttons all the way down her back.

Wait, did I truly see a girl in the forest? I think so. Otherwise, how could I picture her so clearly now, with those old-lady lace-up shoes that seemed so odd for a girl my age? And once again her loneliness sweeps through me like a chilly breeze. If anybody ever needed a friend . . .

I'm lucky. I have Luisa and Sara, but I know them so well that I can predict what they're going to say, like when you see a time-delay on TV and lip-read the words before you hear them. *Bor*ing. I've gone to schools with the same kids forever, in preschool, elementary, and now middle school. Bor*ing*. I've lived here in Dalton all my life. I have been exactly nowhere. Oh, yeah, across the border into Tennessee to visit Ruby Falls, which is forty miles away. *Boring.* My family's okay, I love them all, but they're so *themselves.* Nothing new ever happens, especially when you're the Middle Button and practically invisible in your own family. I'm feeling . . . What am I feeling? Sorry for myself, on my own birthday. Super bored and, let's face it, a little bit lonely. Like Cady.

Her words echo in my mind, as though she's whispering them over my shoulder: *I have been waiting for you . . . waiting for you . . . waiting for you.*

But maybe it's the other way around. Have I been waiting for *her*?

CHAPTER FIVE

"HANNAH? YOU TUNED OUT THERE FOR A MINUTE," Dad says, and Mom automatically puts her palm to my forehead to check for fever. That is so predictably *mother*.

Franny scans the whole crew around our huge oak table as she jams her pie plate into the dishwasher. "Only seventy-two more days until I. AM. OUT. OF. HERE. I could die of boredom before I get to college."

Trick shouts, "Ouch! Quit biting my foot, Gracie. You think you're a cocker spaniel?"

Dad reaches under the table and swoops Gracie up onto his lap. She's cute with her little tufts of straight black hair scrunched into two ponytail horns, but she's as spoiled as last month's milk.

Mom wipes her soapy hands down her sides and shouts to Dad over all the voices, "Our middle girl is twelve now, honey. Remember the day she was born? What a scorcher it was, and our AC had just gone out." She glances over at me. "Hannah went for a long walk by herself tonight. After dark." She's worried because there's nowhere to walk around here for an hour except in the woods.

Dad says, "Hannah, you weren't tramping around in the forest, were you? I've warned you and Scooter about that."

"Who, me?" Scooter says, striking an innocent pose.

Franny groans. "Don't tell me it's time for the Forest Primeval warning."

She fakes a vampirey voice: "You chickadees shall wander forever in the woods, on a night as black as tar, with grapefruit-sized hail pounding through the trees . . ."

"Wouldn't that hail turn the black night white?" Trick asks.

"Details. And hooting owls and swooping hawks . . ."

"Caw! Caw!" Scooter hollers.

I'm thinking of the "Tyger Tyger" poem. "And suddenly the tiger leaps out . . ."

"Alfonso, that's the tiger's name," Scooter declares.

"He's a Bengal tiger from India, you moron," says Trick.

Gracie asks, "Is he a girl?"

"Sure, why not?" Franny continues, "So, Lakshmee, the Bengal she-tiger, leaps out from behind a towering pine tree . . ."

Trick jumps in, "And bares her teeth, those razor-sharp fangs . . ."

Gracie's searching Dad's face for reassurance. They're all thinking *forest* and *tiger,* and *fangs,* but they're not thinking *Cady,* like I am.

I flash Scooter a signal. He swipes his finger through the pie plate and sucks off raspberry goo. "Okay if I go upstairs? I'm on the last chapter of a Percy Jackson book."

"Sure, kid," Mom says. She calls us *baby* and *kid* a lot because otherwise she runs through all our names until she gets to the right one.

"I'm going up for a shower before Franny hogs the bathroom," I quickly add, and I follow Scooter out of the kitchen. The noise behind us, with everybody talking at once, is like a badly tuned school orchestra.

Scooter and I aren't halfway up the winding stairs to our third-floor rooms when I say, "You'll never in a zillion years guess what happened in the forest tonight."

"Uh, a gigantic cigar-shaped space capsule landed in Pukey Pond?"

"Not even close. I met this girl about my age. I didn't see her or hear her, she just suddenly appeared. Scared me so much my heart skipped about eighty beats. She said her name's Cady, and then she just . . . vanished!"

Scooter stops in the middle of the stairs. "Sure, I'm gonna believe *that.*" He's a doubter, but he's a nice one. He sits on the top step, catching his breath. "Okay, go ahead. Describe this mysterious Cady person."

"Old-fashioned, with shoes that you'd see on a covered-wagon girl who's picking wild onions out on the prairie. And she's chalky-pale, like she doesn't get out much."

"You saying she lives in the forest like a wild animal?"

"Maybe." Though she mentioned school. Hmm. The saying *raised by wolves* crosses my mind. I describe the long dress, the tree twigs in her hair, her eyes that change from dim to burning-bright. Like the tiger.

Scooter's eyes are closed, as if he's letting me paint a picture in his head. He has a great imagination. He spends a lot of time reading because his asthma acts up when he runs around too much, and then he doubles over, gasping for breath.

"I'm starting to see her." He's scanning the image in his mind.

"Then maybe you're ready for this. She knew my name."

"Wow, that's creepy!"

"That's not all."

His blue eyes pop open expectantly.

I hesitate, because once the next words are out of my mouth, Scooter and I are in this together up to our nostrils. "She told me, 'I've been waiting for you, Hannah-in-the-Middle.'"

"Whoa!"

"Whoa for sure. So, you have to come with me and see her for yourself."

"Tomorrow after lunch. Because p.m. is better than a.m. for my stupid lungs."

"Okay, but you can't tell the family."

He laughs. "You kidding? They'll think *I'm* crazy like you."

CHAPTER SIX

SCOOTER AND I CAN'T GO TO THE WOODS AFTER lunch on Friday because it's Mom and Dad's weekly date for lunch and a movie, so I'm stuck babysitting Gracie. But at least it's for actual money. No way I'm passing that up. My piggy bank needs dollars to buy this purse in the shape of a blue dolphin. Blue is so my color, and dolphins are awesome, super-intelligent creatures. If I weren't a human, I'd want to be a dolphin — except I'm not a great swimmer.

So it isn't until Saturday that we can head out. We plan to leave early. I love getting up at six a.m., when the whole day spreads out in front of me full of possibilities — or it does when I have friends around. Sigh. Anyway, this is the hour when normal people turn over in bed and hit the snooze button to catch a few more snores, but I'm ready to conquer a beautiful summer day. If we're lucky, the temperature won't climb higher than ninety in the shade. Scooter's feeling great this morning. Whatever was growing yesterday was washed out by the heavy rain, so his allergies haven't kicked up. We're dressed in shorts and tees, spritzed with bug spray, smeared with sunblock, and we're tiptoeing out the back door to find Cady.

"Bet she won't be there," he says, hustling to keep up with me. "Bet you made her up just to freak me out."

"Would I do such a thing?"

"Yeah!"

We've reached the fallen log that blocks easy access to the forest, and we practically leap over it. "A little farther," I say. "Just keep walking. Here, this is where I saw her sitting on that stone bench right in front of —"

"Nobody's on the bench."

"Let's keep going, maybe she's doing some exploring," I tell Scooter. "Cady?" I call loud enough to knock a bird out of a tree. "Caa-dee! My brother Scooter's here to meet you." We look behind thick tree trunks and bushes in case she's hiding from us as a joke to pop out and yell *boo!* I hate when someone sneaks up on me. Shading my eyes, I gaze off beyond Moonlight Lake, hoping for some movement in the brush that isn't a wild animal. I'm sure she'll be running toward us in those old-lady shoes. I'm determined to prove to Scooter, and myself, that I'm not a lunatic, and Cady actually exists.

"It's bear cub season," Scooter says. "If a mama bear spots us, she'll go wild to protect her babies, like our fierce mom does. Say a brown bear smells bacon on us and we're the first fresh meat she sees smack out of three months of hibernation, and she weighs, like, a thousand pounds. We're just peanuts and Cracker Jacks to her and her cubs."

"You are such a pessimist, Scooter. Why did I even bring you here?"

"To meet the imaginary Cady," he reminds me, arching his skinny eyebrows.

Cady, who is nowhere in sight. I call her name again, north, south, east, and west, but there's no response except for two round eyes peering out at us from inside a tree burrow. Cady? Stuffed in a tree? No! It's a raccoon, curious about us giant creatures tramping around in his forest.

My shoulders sag. "We might as well go home," I say in defeat.

"Guess that bear's gonna have to find some other junk food," says Scooter. "Cady might be a tasty snack."

Scooter's the only one who can tease me this way without my getting mad.

"Come on, Hannah, let's go home and have breakfast," Scooter says, and he leads me, a little too eagerly, out of the forest. We've been here so many times. This time? Scooter won't admit it, but I think he senses something creepy in the forest this morning, like I do.

I just wish Cady had shown up so I could introduce her to Scooter. He and I are really close, which doesn't stop me from playing tricks on him, so no wonder he thinks I made Cady up. The clouds have rolled in, and we're fixin' for a big old summer storm. Second time this week. We make it into the mudroom of Nightshade just as the sky cracks open.

If you like a clashing, crashing thunderstorm, which I do, the best place to watch it happen is from Dad's studio. I love the sound of the rain pinging the roof and pattering on the windows on all three sides. Dad's deep in concentration working on elevation details for a public library he's designing in Polk County. I'm tracing the rain streaking down the window, my finger guessing which direction it's going to jump to.

There's a knock on Dad's door. "Joe? Sally sent me right up to have a look at that balcony." It's Mac Mosely, a contractor whose carpentry crew does a lot of building for Dad. "Couldn't have picked a worse day, all that cloudburst out there, but at least I can eye the structure and come back when it's dried up."

Mr. Mosely makes me think of a flagpole. He's more than six and a half feet tall, with a thick mop of gray hair that's waving in the breeze of the air conditioner. Looking out through the glass door while sucking on a toothpick, he says with a hearty chuckle, "That platform sure is leanin' south. All that water's not helpin'."

Mr. Mosely inspects the glass door leading to the balcony and pries a fat blade between the wall and the doorframe. "Painted shut, mebbe six layers deep, some of 'em going back years." He keeps prying and chipping. Paint slivers dot the floor. "Somebody meant for this door to be shut up for good, Joe. Under all that paint, there's nails about every two inches. Gonna have to get my guys out here to rip the door out and rebuild the whole dang balcony, else it could snap off like a dead twig and mash anything below it. A kid playing in the yard, worst case."

Dad and Mr. Mosely work out the details of when and how much — busy summer, can't get to it for a couple of weeks, it'll cost lots of money — while I'm left wondering why the people who lived in Nightshade before us were so determined that no one would ever go out that door. Was that after the balcony started *leanin' south*, or before?

Later, when Mr. Mosely's gone, it's still pouring out there and the house is unusually quiet. Trick went to a movie — some gross thing I wouldn't be caught dead at — and Gracie's riding her wooden tricycle up and down the second floor hallway. Mom believes in *projects* during the summer — no daytime TV and no hanging out on the computer, even on rainy days. She's got Scooter and me set up with a dorky art activity involving colored kaleidoscopic stencils and multicolored tapes, so I know we'll be bored to death in ten minutes, max.

If I can't go back to the forest, I'm itching to stir up some ruckus. "I have a diabolical idea, Scooter!"

"Oh, great," he mutters, but I know he's game for anything I toss his way.

CHAPTER SEVEN

"YOU KNOW HOW WE'RE ALWAYS SAYING THAT Nightshade is haunted?" Not that I believe in ghosts, but it's a great way to put some chill into a day muggy enough for steam to form inside our windows. I stash Mom's art project stencils in a box and lead Scooter to the broom closet on the second floor. "Scooter Flynn, put this day down in history. I'm telling you, this is where the Ghost of Nightshade lives."

He looks at me as if I've grown a second nose on my chin. "Give it up, Hannah. You've already tried to fool me with that Cady thing."

"I wasn't tricking you. And this is way different." I throw open the closet door. "Ta-da!"

He peers into the dark mess of mops and buckets, smelling like a sickly mixture of dust and ammonia. "I don't see any ghosts."

"You don't *see* them because they're invisible. They're out to lunch now, but I know where they hide."

"No way."

"Oh, yeah? Come in here." I shove aside the sweeper and oily rags and lead Scooter into the murky cave of the closet. "Watch this." I mash a tiny button, and the inside wall slides open. "Told you!"

"Holy cow, Hannah." Scooter sticks his head into the space behind the wall. "How did you find this?" his echoey voice asks. "But it doesn't prove anything about ghosts or ghouls."

"Maybe not, but I sure had you going there, didn't I?"

He backs out of the secret space, and scrunches up his lips as if he's about to kiss a tarantula. "Nah, not even for a second."

Then I hear the whistly sound in his chest. "Lotta dust or mold in there," he says shallowly.

We back out of the closet, tripping over Gracie on her tricycle.

She grins. "Gracie hide there, too!"

"No, Gracie, too spooky," I warn her, slamming and re-locking the closet door. Scooter knocks toys to the floor and drops into the rocking chair. Most people breathe without thinking about it, in and out, quiet and smooth. For Scooter, it's different. His shoulders rise and fall as he struggles for air.

"You okay? I'll get Mom." Her office door is open a little. The clattering of her printer says she's working on her

"Dear Bettina" column, which means Do Not Disturb Unless the House is Engulfed in Flames.

"Don't bug her," Scooter says. "I'm okay. Just . . . need . . . to catch my breath."

I know better. I should *never* have sent him into that closet where all that dust and cleaning stuff triggered his asthma. He's doubled over, and his chest pumps like a panting dog's. Hardly any air is hitting his lungs. I know the routine and fumble in his pocket for his inhaler: "Okay, Scooter, sit up straight. Take deep, slow breaths. In . . . out . . . in . . . out . . . in . . . out." I shake the inhaler and hold it at his mouth. Three puffs, pause, shake, three more puffs. "You're doing great." Except he's not. His face is the color of a whale: blue-gray.

"Mom!" I screech, and she gets it right away, and bounds out of her office. She firmly pushes Scooter against the back of the rocking chair, tilting his chin up to open an airway. "Keep going, honey. Deep, slow breaths, that a boy. You're coming around." After about twelve more jagged in-and-outs, Mom says, "You're my hero. You're over the hump." She shoulders away her tears of terror, which she only allows when the worst is over.

I run for a cool washcloth for the beads of sweat dropping from Scooter's forehead. "This stinks, doesn't it?" He just nods; it's too hard to talk. In a little while, Mom morphs into "Dear Bettina" again and returns to her office, but she leaves the door wide open just in case.

Oh, Gracie! I forgot about her witnessing this whole thing. She's smashed against the wall, clutching her panda and chewing the inside of her lip. Inching forward, she asks, "Okay, Shooter?" Then lays her head in his lap until his face pinks up. Gracie's like a pup who senses when her human's in trouble. Maybe she *is* part cocker spaniel, like Trick said.

⚘ ◉ ⚘

The afternoon clears up, and though it's going to be a muddy bog in the forest, and I'll be soaked by rain dribbling off the wet trees, I *have* to go back just to prove to myself that Cady exists. Franny's working her shift at the Rib Shack today, and Trick is at baseball practice on the soggy field at Edwards Park. Mom and Dad are both working, Mom pounding keys in her office, and Dad in his third-floor architecture studio. It's the perfect time to sneak away. But then . . .

"Hannah," Mom calls from behind her office door. "Do me a favor, honey. Put Gracie down for her nap, please. Round up a sippy cup of milk, her blankie, and her panda, and read her a book."

"Aw, Mom, do I have to?" I am *not* Gracie's mother. Why should I have to put her to bed when I desperately want to get back to the woods?

Mom frowns at her office door, waving pages hot off the printer. "Scooter can help if he's feeling okay."

He's downstairs, bouncing back from his asthma attack. He shouldn't be climbing all those stairs yet.

"Never mind, I'll do it," I whine. "Come on, Gracie, storybook time."

"Storybook!" Gracie flies down the hall. It's lots easier to fool her into a nap than to fool Scooter into thinking there is truly a girl named Cady in the woods.

I rock Gracie a while and plunk her into her crib with her lovies and run downstairs to where Scooter's sprawled on the sofa with three stiff foam pillows behind him. Without even looking up from his Harry Potter book, he says, "What are you fixin' to do about this Cady thing?" That's Scooter, always getting right to the point, as though he hasn't got time to mess around like regular people do. He's a lot older than eleven on the inside.

"Think I should go back and look for her?"

Scooter shrugs. "Depends. Do you *want* to find her?"

"I don't know how to answer that."

Another page flips by. I wish I could read as fast as he does.

"If you don't know whether you want to find her," Scooter says, "maybe you should just hang around here in Nightshade like a scared rat."

"I'm no kind of rodent, scared or otherwise. I am a woman who will make history!"

Scooter continues reading while he talks. "You're Rosa Parks. You're Anne Frank. Hey, you're the Queen of Sheba."

"I don't have to be them. I'm me, Hannah Flynn. Now put that book down! You've read it six times already."

He tents the book across his stomach and gives me one of his penetrating wise-old-man looks. "Hermione would go looking in the forest."

"I wish you could come with me. I'm positive Cady will turn up this time."

"Tomorrow, or the next day." He hides behind the book again, which tells me that he's not quite back to his old self yet.

"I'm going, with or without you. Don't tell Mom."

Three fingers slide up from the top of the book. "Scout's honor."

So I'm off into the forest, a message looping in my head over and over: Is it possible that I imagined Cady when it was dark and scary and strangely cold for a humid summer evening? That I invented her the way I just invented myself as the Ghost of Nightshade?

CHAPTER EIGHT

A SQUIRREL FLIPS HIS TAIL FROM A TREE LIMB AT MY eye level. He's clutching an acorn, his yummy lunch, between tiny paws. He glares at me as if he's saying, "I'm home. What are *you* doing here?"

I slip between trees into the clearing. Pine needles crunch under my sandals as I move toward the lake. The humid air smells swampy. About twenty feet ahead of me, Moonlight Lake glimmers serenely in the midday sun. It's so beautiful, so inviting, dappled with drops of water from a tree that hangs over the south shore of the lake. Cady's here somewhere, I know it. In anticipation, my nerves tighten like guitar strings thrumming along with the insect song in the giant trees all around me.

How weird! The tamped down path and stone bench are both gone. My heart sinks with disappointment. Or am I in the wrong part of the forest that I thought I knew so well?

There's no sign of Cady anywhere. And then suddenly there she is, peeking around the large trunk of a pine, but she looks totally different.

"Hi!" Cady shouts. "You look surprised. You came here looking for me, didn't you?"

"Yes, but you don't look the same — the cut-offs, the T-shirt, the flip-flops."

"I changed clothes." Pointing to my blue cotton shift with the spaghetti straps, she says, "So did you, look at you." She sounds angry. Why?

Yesterday I wore cut-off jean shorts and that oversized T-shirt. Today's a lot hotter, and dresses are airy and cooler. Why should she care what I wear?

Her smile lights up the forest. "I just want us to be friends. See?" She pulls out the lower corners of her T-shirt so I can read the message: A WOMAN'S PLACE IS IN THE HOUSE AND THE SENATE.

That echoes the shirt Sara and Luisa gave me.

"Friendship, that's what counts, not the clothes we wear," Cady says.

Really? Then why is she copying my clothes? At least her hair's different from mine, an ashy brown still held on top of her head with those weird twigs, and curly around her cheeks. Mine's dark and hangs down my back with some annoying waves that I'm always trying to straighten into Selena Gomez hair. Also, all that hair is sweaty. Maybe I should put my hair up like Cady does.

I crack the awkward silence between us. "If we're friends, shouldn't I know your last name?"

"Emerson? Conover? Gutierrez? Choose the one that fits me best."

I tuck my hair behind my ears, which I do when I'm nervous or I'm not sure what to say. "That makes no sense, Cady. Besides, you still haven't told me where you come from and why you're here in my forest."

"Your forest! Oh, that's hilarious." She throws her head back and offers a deep, throaty laugh. Some animal pokes out of a hollow in a tree trunk to see what's going on. "A raccoon." She answers the question I haven't even asked, then leans over and pets the raccoon's head and gently lifts out one of its babies, as cute and helpless as a newborn puppy.

"Adorable! Can I hold it?"

Cady pulls the raccoon away, lays it back into the tree-hollow den, and says, "Raccoons carry rabies and lots of other diseases that hurt humans."

"You're human. You're not afraid."

Her pale eyes dim for a few seconds as she thinks that over. "Natural immunity. I suppose it's because I live here; they know me," she explains.

"Live *where*, exactly?"

Cady motions vaguely to someplace beyond the lake and invites me to sit beside her in a nest of soft pine needles.

While I pluck away at a pinecone (he loves me, he loves me not, the *he* being adorable Garrett Flume), she turns to grab a picnic basket. For a flash of a second it seems her whole body in profile is as flat as a ruler. Must be the trees' shadows playing tricks on my eyes, because when she turns to me again, she's solid. A small rectangular bulge in her pocket is probably a phone.

And then I automatically tap my own phone pocket, which doesn't exist in my sundress, and realize, one, that I don't have my phone with me, and two, even if I did, I wouldn't be able to call for help if I were in trouble because the reception out here is nonexistent.

I'm *not* in trouble. Cady is harmless. She holds the picnic basket on her lap. It's the kind with lids that flap open on either side of the handle. She lifts the side farthest from me so I can't see what's in it.

"Hungry?" She reaches into the basket.

"What have you got? Oh, by the way, I told my brother Scooter about you."

"Why did you do that?" Cady snaps, slamming the picnic basket shut.

Boy, she's moody, but I can be just as snarky. "Because I tell him everything. Well, everything that's important to me. But Scooter doesn't believe you exist. He thinks you're another one of my dumb tricks."

"Well, it just proves that Scooter Flynn doesn't know everything. So, are we friends, Hannah-in-the-Middle?"

"Don't call me that. I hate it."

She nods with a faraway look, as if she's sifting through mental folders to file away this piece of info. What a strange girl!

"I understand what you're saying about the middle thing," Cady begins, "because I come from a big family, like you. A smart girl can be lost in a messy mob like that."

"Yes!" That's something Sara and Luisa just don't get, because there are only two kids in their families, not a whole tribe. They love the stop-and-go circus at Nightshade. Finally, somebody who understands me. Suddenly, I open like a sunflower.

Honestly, it's not like me to be such a chatterbox. Mom's always having to coax me to talk. But she's Mom; friends are different. I guess I'm missing Luisa and Sara, even though they just left yesterday. So before I know it, I'm blathering a mile a minute, and Cady's listening as if she's memorizing every detail, in case of a pop quiz.

CHAPTER NINE

WHILE CADY STRIPS THE STALKS OF A BUNCH OF leaves, my mouth keeps running at warp speed.

"My older sister Franny has these amazing long, colt-like legs. She looks fabulous in skinny jeans. But my legs are short, and I'm short-waisted, built more like my dad, so I wear dresses a lot. Jeans make me look stubby, and dresses are cooler in the summer anyway." I stop suddenly, embarrassed that I'm rattling on so shamelessly. Cady gives me a spin of her hand that says, *tell me more.*

"My mother and father both have offices at home. My dad's an architect, so he travels to the site of wherever he's building. Franny is the only one of us old enough to drive, but she works at the Rib Shack a bunch of hours, so she can't take me anywhere. That dumps a lot of responsibility for my sister Gracie on my shoulders because Scooter has bad allergies and gets sick a lot, and my brother Trick is obsessed with baseball. It's all he talks about and thinks about. He divides the food on his plate into first base, second, third, and home. I am so totally not a jock. It doesn't matter to me whether the Atlanta Braves win a game, or even show up to play, or whether Trick gets to home plate at dinner."

"Same for me. Baseball, ugh." Cady gazes at me, raises her eyebrows, encouraging more, which I give.

"The thing about my sister Franny is that she just graduated, and she's leaving at the end of summer. Going to college in Athens."

"Athens?" Cady asks with alarm.

"Not Athens, Greece. Athens, Georgia, where the university is. I thought everybody knew that." Where has she been? On Pluto?

Again, I sense that Cady's filing this information.

"Franny's a pain in the rear most of the time. She can't wait to leave home, but I don't want that time to come, ever. If you have an older sister, you know what I'm saying. Do you have one you hate and love at the same time?"

"Yes. No."

"Which?"

"I can't say," she replies, tilting her head as if she truly doesn't know.

"Isn't that a little fact you'd remember about your family?"

Quick as an eye blink, she changes the subject. "Tell me about your friends. Besides me."

A big sigh. "Luisa and Sara, my two best friends, are gone for the next few weeks. So's everyone else I usually hang out with. They're all at music camp, riding camp, or on exciting trips. One friend, Barb, stays with her father on a dude ranch in Montana all summer. Scooter's *it*. But he's a good it."

"Scooter," Cady mutters. "Little brothers are a pain." She pats my sweaty hand with my chipped blue nail polish. Franny usually does my manis and pedis, but she's been too busy with final exams and graduation and her boyfriend, Cameron, and now her job. *And she's leaving in August.*

Cady's hand is unnaturally cold, like she's been juggling ice cubes, though today's hot enough to fry an egg on the boulder I'm leaning against.

"Bless your heart, you're feeling a little lonely, aren't you?" Cady says. "You don't have to be. You have me, now, and I have lots of friends close by." She motions toward that same vague area beyond the lake.

I shift my eyes toward the water. "Don't you just love Moonlight Lake? I do. Here's something hilarious. Scooter calls that beautiful lake Pukey Pond. That's a guy, for you!"

Cady's eyebrows nearly meet in a frown. She doesn't like him? Everybody loves Scooter. She's never even met him. Maybe she's insulted by the Pukey Pond thing.

"I'll see if my friends would like to meet you," she says, after a long pause.

"Sounds great." Who could she be talking about? I know *every* girl in Dalton between the ages of seven and seventeen. "You don't mean boys, do you?"

"No, no! Girls our age. You'd like them, I know you would."

Sheesh, I hope she doesn't spill all my family secrets to her friends.

"They're a little shy about meeting a new person unless they're sure she can be an honest and true friend." She stares into my eyes, and I feel an electric charge zap through me. "Are you honest and true, Hannah?"

"I am! I'm the most honest and true person alive!"

"I believe that's the truth," Cady says.

"Scooter thinks I'm —"

She interrupts me. "Come back tomorrow."

"If it's not pouring."

"Wear rain boots."

"Yes, but —"

"I'll be here. Will you?" she says abruptly.

Boy, talk about rude! She listens like I'm the most fascinating girl since Katniss Everdeen (without the bow and arrow), then cuts me off cold. And that picnic basket. What's that all about? She asked if I was hungry, but never offered me goodies from the basket, which she slammed shut before I could peek inside.

What's in that basket that she doesn't want me to see?

CHAPTER TEN

THE NEXT MORNING, I DON'T WASTE A MILLISECOND between breakfast and whatever Mom has in store for me, and I sprint back to the woods. This time Cady's waiting for me just inside the entrance to the forest.

"You been standing here since I left yesterday?"

"No, just hoping you'd come this morning. Let's go." She weaves in and out of trees on bare feet, and I hurry to keep up, until we get to a nice, sunny clearing. She's prepared it with soft leaves, which I sure hope aren't poison ivy.

"What do you want to do?" she asks.

"I don't know. Hide-and-seek?"

"It wouldn't be fair. I know these woods lots better than you do. I'd find you before you could say OMG."

It's peaceful sitting here on these soft leaves, with my chin on my knees. For once, we're dressed the same — Old Navy shorts and button-down shirts. Mom thinks it's indecent to have these measly two inches of skin showing, so I don't tie the knot above my waist until I'm out of her X-ray vision.

"I know! Let's play Truth or Dare," Cady says, tying her shirt just like mine. She tucks her long hair behind her ears like I do. In fact, we look so much alike now that we could be sisters, or at least first cousins.

"Sure!" I've played this game a million times at sleepovers.

Cady drags a twig into the center of the leaves between us and spins it, which I never do for Truth or Dare, but whatever. The twig misses both of us, but a squirrel is watching us, maybe trying to figure out the rules of the game. "Okay, squirrel, choose: truth or dare?"

"I don't think she gets it. Spin again." This time it points to me.

"Truth or dare?"

"Truth." I might regret this!

"Have you ever kissed a boy?"

"On the cheek once at the sixth-grade picnic. It was a boy named Garrett Flume." I feel my face flush at just the mention of his name. "Do you know him from school?"

She shakes her head.

"Garrett Flume had those tiny rubber band things connecting his upper and lower braces, and he opened his mouth so wide when my lips connected with his cheek that all the rubber bands snapped. Poor guy was so shocked that he swallowed a mouthful of rubber."

Cady has a great laugh. It feels so good to laugh together

with a new friend who doesn't already know every detail of my whole life.

I spin the twig, rigging it so it points to Cady. "Truth or dare?"

"Truth."

"What's your last name?"

"Dare," she says quickly.

"Um, okay, I dare you to twist yourself into a pretzel."

No problem. She can practically wrap her foot around her neck. Maybe she should try out for the Olympic gymnastics team.

"Your turn," she says, spinning the twig. "Truth or dare?"

"Truth."

"Am I your best friend now?" Cady studies my face so boldly that I have to look away. "Dare."

"Fair enough," Cady says. "Okay, I dare you to wade into Moonlight Lake up to your navel."

I'm thinking sinkholes, snakes, spidery webs like Dad warned, but, like I always say, women who behave . . . I jump up, kick off my flip-flops, and run toward the lake. The first step sinks me into wet sand, and I nearly lose my balance. Then the water welcomes me and eddies around me like a silky cocoon. It is so *not* Pukey Pond.

"Come back," Cady calls to me, and though I don't

really want to get out, I drag myself back to the shore. I'll never be afraid of Moonlight Lake again.

Soaked through to my underwear, it's not comfortable on the bed of leaves anymore.

"Fun, but I gotta get home. Mom's paying me to babysit Gracie while she goes to the library to research something for 'Dear Bettina.'"

"Who's Bettina?"

"She's like 'Dear Abby,' only funnier." Cady looks totally puzzled. "You never read advice to the lovelorn and the crazies of the world? It's the only thing worth reading in the newspaper. Do you live under a rock?"

"Yeah, I kind of do," she says. "Tomorrow?"

"If I can."

"Tomorrow!" she says, like it's an order I can't refuse. That's okay. Tomorrow I'm coming back with Scooter. He and Cady are gonna love each other. Maybe.

At home, Gracie's down for her nap, and I'm filing Dad's papers in his studio. It's my other summer job, which earns me about twenty-five cents an hour. Even prisoners make more than that working in the steamy jail kitchen. But, as Mom is always reminding me, it's another one of my family responsibilities. Each of us five kids has jobs, even Gracie, who's supposed to slide everybody's dirty sheets down the laundry shoot on Tuesdays.

"Hi, Mr. Mosely!" I call as the carpenter comes into the studio.

He waves his clipboard toward me in greeting and turns to Dad. "Like I said on the phone, Joe, we'll start tearing up the balcony pretty soon. Just wanted to show y'all a couple of dicey things about it." He spreads the Nightshade blueprints out on Dad's drafting table.

"See, thing is, the balcony wasn't in the original blueprints. House was built in 1895, balcony not until 1897. I went down to the City and got the permits. It was shoddy work, Joe. Somebody did a rush job, so no wonder it gave out. That floor out there now?" He leads Dad to the glass door, and I peer around them. "Put in later, I'd say maybe 1940, but the workmen didn't have pride in their work. Look how it leans."

Dad nods in agreement, and then Mr. Mosely totally surprises me.

"Say, while we're workin' on the new balcony, want my guys to dig you a pool? Used to be one right there, under the balcony."

Now it's a vegetable garden. Who wouldn't trade carrots and turnips for a pool, especially on a day as hot and sticky as this one? "What happened to the swimming pool, Mr. Mosely?"

"Filled in with tons of dirt. By the way, it wasn't a swimmin' pool. It was what ya call a reflectin' pool. Meant to reflect the house. Water only about twofoot deep. But if y'all are wantin' a backyard swimmin' hole, I believe my boys can do that."

"Not until Gracie gets older," Dad says, and my hopes sink. That's the way it's been since school let out, a few ups, more downs, and good-byes and disappointments and texts from my friends who are having the time of their lives.

But at least there's Cady.

CHAPTER ELEVEN

"GRACIE! WHERE ARE YOU?" POKING HER HEAD into my room, Mom asks, "Hannah, have you seen your sister?"

"Why do I have to be the one to keep an eye on her?" I grumble.

"We all have a responsibility for one another. It's called family." Not *that* again. It's my signal to pout and follow her down to the second floor to hunt for Gracie, who's probably hiding under her crib with her stuffed panda.

But she's not there.

Mom swishes open the shower curtain in the bathroom. No Gracie. "She was in my office scribbling in her Snow White coloring book a moment ago." Mom raps on Scooter's door. He's belly down on the tile floor, working a crossword puzzle. "Honey, have you seen Gracie?"

"Hunh-uh," he responds, filling in a few squares.

"Scooter, be so kind as to give me your eyeballs," Mom says, and he reluctantly looks up, pencil frozen over the puzzle book.

"Did you try the broom closet?" Scooter offers.

"Why would she go into that skunky space?" asks Mom.

Scooter shoots me a look, and I race downstairs for the closet, Mom following. We push aside the mops and buckets and smelly rags, but there's no sign of Gracie.

Mom's frantic. "Gracie, where are you?"

A tiny, muffled voice says: "Here, Mama."

"I know where." I find the button and the secret wall slides open. There's Gracie smiling in the dark, cradling her panda.

"Oh, baby, you must be so scared! I sure was." Mom scoops Gracie up into her arms.

"No, Mama. Wady talk to me."

Mom gazes into Gracie's face. "A lady?"

Her little head bobs up and down. "Wady say, 'Hi Gracie!'"

We back out of the closet, Mom clutching Gracie to her heart. "You have quite an imagination. Need a snack, baby? Let's go have some Goldfish and peaches."

"Okay." Gracie reaches behind Mom, waving. "Bye-bye, wady."

When the two of them are downstairs, I burst into Scooter's room. "She was in the broom closet."

"Where the ghosts hang out," Scooter teases.

"Yeah, smarty. I think Gracie met one."

"No way!"

"Well, she wasn't a bit scared sitting in the dark with somebody who called her name."

Scooter slams the puzzle book shut. "She must have heard us talking about the imaginary ghosts in there."

"Be realistic. Gracie doesn't have the words to know what a ghost is, even if she heard us talking. And why wasn't she terrified in that dark secret compartment all alone? I think she actually met a lady in there."

"You mean, there really *are* ghosts in this house?"

"No." I pause uncomfortably. "I don't know."

⚜

The next morning I shout down the stairs to the immediate world, "Who took my blue nail polish?"

Trick ducks his head out of the bathroom. "Yeah, I burglarized your room, 'cause Coach wants all us Dalton Devils to do our nails before the next game!"

Scooter's behind him with toothpaste foam covering half his face. "I don' 'ave ut," he mumbles around the toothbrush hanging out of his mouth. He flashes me his chewed fingernail stubs for proof. He spits toothpaste in the sink and says, "It must have been the ghost in the broom closet."

I scowl at him. The yelling wakes Gracie up. I dash back to my room to escape to the attic. Up there I won't hear

Mom shouting from the kitchen for me to get Gracie up, which means dealing with her soggy diaper.

The attic is the best part of the house, where no one bothers me. To get to the attic from my bedroom, you climb on a chair to slide the trap door in the ceiling to the side, then pull down this little ladder. Seven steep, narrow steps, and you're in the attic. It's gloomy and always either too hot, or too cold, and too dusty for Scooter, but I've got legendary lungs.

So I've set up my universe with cushions on the floor under the window and a lamp with a paper shade that turns my corner a soft, muzzy blue. Books and my iPad and a sketch pad and colored pencils are tossed across the floor. I've tucked packages of Oreos and Cheetos and little apple juice boxes on a high ledge so the mice can't get them. I could *live* up here, except there's no bathroom. On days like today, it's the perfect place to curl up on the pillows to read a creepy mystery while rain pings the roof right over my head and slithers down the slanted window in thick rivulets. Up here I'd be the first person in the house to spot a rainbow arcing across the sky when the shy sun peeks out from behind the clouds. Besides the spectacular sky, the view isn't so great because everything below the window is blocked by the balcony that juts out from Dad's studio.

I'm still in my pj's, my back against a battered and scuffed leather trunk that belonged to Dad's grandparents.

"What's in it?" I asked him the day the movers struggled to jam it in through the attic window.

"Just bolts of fabric and ribbon from my grandpa's shop in Thomasville. Hasn't been opened in years. The whole thing would probably fall apart if you tried to jiggle the lock. It's a family heirloom. You know what *heirloom* means, Hannah?" Of course I did, but before I could answer, he said, "It's a thing that's passed from one generation to the next that no one wants, but no one dares get rid of. Be careful; someday it could be yours to lug from house to house," he said, laughing.

The lock doesn't budge. It's probably corroded and needs a slug of oil and maybe a crowbar. Hard work, which I'm feeling too comfy and lazy to do right now.

Gentle thunder rumbles off in the distant mountains, and then it's quiet again, and *The Case of the Spinning Acrobat* captures me. It's the third book in the Haunted Circus series. I can't wait to dig into it. But what's that noise? Skittering mice? I glance up at my stash on the ledge; no critters. Anyway, it sounds more like someone sliding a palm across nubby paper. A breeze flutters past me, chilling the sweat on my back. A draft from a tiny hole in the roof? I look up. It's pitch-black up there, but then a sudden burst of lightning illuminates crisscrossed wooden rafters that look like huge dinosaur bones.

Wait, there's that sound again. Now it's like someone tiptoeing in soft slippers. I spin around. No one's there. My eyes explore the shifting shadows of boxes stacked along the wall, a crate of toys Gracie's outgrown, an antique gramophone broken and leaning into an armchair oozing its white stuffing. On a small three-legged table stands a huge silver teapot covered in crackly plastic, another one of those *heirlooms* that nobody wants. I do a double-take in the distant corner and jump, seeing a thin man with a derby hat angled on his head. Whew, no, it's a hat rack, just a hat rack.

I have loved this attic since the day we moved into Nightshade. I've always felt safe and comfy up here. Today? Something's different. A ripple of fear snakes up my back, across my shoulders. What's scaring me? The pounding rain, the dark clouds, the gloomy shadows? It's enough to make me snatch up my mystery and iPad. With a bag of Cheetos dangling from my teeth, I scamper down the ladder. Now that I'm twelve, maybe I've outgrown the attic just like Gracie outgrew the toys stored in the crate.

Or maybe there *is* something creepy up there, just like there is in the broom closet.

CHAPTER TWELVE

GRACIE IS WRANGLING HER WAY OUT OF THE
Food Lion kid seat. She's always hyper in the cereal aisle,
trying to grab any cartoony box she can reach. Franny
tosses Cocoa Puffs into the cart, and that calms Gracie
for a while.

"Mom will have a fit," I remind Franny. Sugary cereals
are a no-no at Nightshade.

We round the corner into the canned veggies aisle, and
there's Cady, deeply concentrating on a can of asparagus
spears. Who buys white asparagus spears? I mean, really?

"Hi, Cady."

"Oh, Hannah! You shop at Food Lion, too? These
your sisters? Let's see, you're Gracie," she says, jiggling
Gracie's big toe. "And you're Franny, the one who's counting down the days 'til you leave the cozy family nest and
run away to college. You're going to break Hannah's heart,
you know."

Franny's eyes flare, and I shoot Cady a glare that could
raise fiery blisters on her nose. I'm hugely embarrassed

and furious. So much for telling a friend something in confidence.

Franny coolly studies Cady. "Live around here? I've never seen you before. What school do you go to?" Uh-oh, here's the interrogation, but Cady's earned it.

She laughs, then claps her hand to her mouth, I think to hide crooked bottom teeth. I can't help but notice that she's wearing blue nail polish. Sheesh, is she trying to be *me*?

She says, "No, you haven't seen me before, and yes, I live near your house, and no, I don't go to a Dalton school anymore. My friends and I have our own home school. Y'all learn things to pass a test. We learn things that stick with you for a lifetime." She mutters something under her breath that I don't catch.

Franny makes a sharp U-turn, pushing the cart and Gracie out of the aisle. The whole scene is totally embarrassing. "We gotta run," I offer over my shoulder, and that sure doesn't explain Franny's rudeness, or Cady's.

Wouldn't you know it? Cady ends up right behind us in the checkout line. She hands Gracie a bag of M&Ms.

"Fanks!" Gracie cries, meaning she and Cady are now best friends for life.

"Not 'til after dinner." Franny snatches the bag out of Gracie's hands.

In a huff, Cady takes off. She stomps on the rubber mat to activate the automatic door and hurries outside.

It occurs to me that Cady had no groceries in her shopping cart. Wait, no shopping cart, either! I look for her in the parking lot. Someone must have driven her here. It's way too far to walk from where she lives. Wherever she lives. There's no sign of her. She must have gone back into the store through a different entrance. Does she just hang out at Food Lion for fun? I can think of lots of places I'd rather be on a summery afternoon — horseback riding at Fort Mountain State Park, swimming at Dad's club. Definitely *not* sweating my head off at Trick's baseball game — which is where we're heading later today.

And my face is burning with embarrassment. While I'm loading groceries into the back, and Franny's buckling Gracie into the car seat, Franny lets me have it.

"How could you embarrass me that way, Hannah? What happens at Nightshade stays at Nightshade. I thought I could trust you."

"You can. I'm really sorry. I just . . . well, there's no excuse. Cady listens to me, and my friends are all off having awesome summers, and I have no one else around." It's lame, but it's the best I can do as I slam the back gate and slide into the seat next to Franny.

"You used to talk to me," Franny says, and the only sound in the car all the way home is Gracie singing "itsy bitsy spider."

At home, I'm feeling like a worm for letting Franny down, but I'm also mad that my new *friend* would do such a mean thing. "Mom, okay if I don't go to Trick's game? I'm hot and sweaty and just want to chill at home."

"Sure, honey, I understand. You need more *me* time, less *us* time. You've always been that way. It's a middle child thing, isn't it? Trick's not pitching today, anyway, so it could be a yawner."

Perfect! Because while the family's gone, and Cady's lurking around in the Food Lion parking lot until somebody (who?) comes to pick her up, I'm going to go exploring in the woods without her watchful eyes.

I'm drawn to Moonlight Lake. It's so captivating and mysterious. There's a foggy mist hanging just over the water as I arrive. Kicking off my flip-flops, I push aside a cluster of marsh marigolds and drop to the soft bank of the lake, dunking my heels into the cool water that's irresistible and refreshing on this boiling, sticky day. My toes tangle in a web under the surface of the lake. "Sorry to disturb your handiwork, Ms. Spider," I murmur. Doubt if she hears me. A dragonfly lazily circles a bed of water lilies floating just out of my reach. On the west side of the lake a mama duck leads a parade of her ducklings. So peaceful, so beautiful.

The sun burns off the misty fog, revealing a small cabin on the north bank of the lake. I've got to see what that's about, so I jump to my feet and forge my way through the marshy bushes toward the hut, with my flip-flops hooked over my thumb. If Cady can go barefoot in the forest, so can I.

Ouch! This isn't as easy as it looks. Something just went squish. Hopping along, I check out the victim stuck to my foot. A centipede. I scrape the disgusting thing off on a rock and trot toward the cabin, but as I get closer, my nerves kick in. What if there's someone inside? Oh, who'd be in there besides Cady and her friends? But still, they wouldn't like me barging in like an invader, so I knock. No answer. I stand on tiptoes to peek in the window, which has no glass. The cabin's empty. Opening the door slowly, I'm ready to hurl my shoes at any animal that comes barreling out.

I have to duck my head to get inside this broken-down hut. Three small, battered beach chairs, with slats painted red and yellow and green, form a circle in the center of the one room. What kind of friends does Cady have that would fit in such Gracie-sized chairs? Elves? Leprechauns? Give me a break! Or maybe all of her friends are under the age of three. Now I'm more curious than ever to meet her *honest and true* friends.

CHAPTER THIRTEEN

"READY TO GO?" A FEW DAYS LATER, I'M ITCHING to return to the woods. I put my ear to Scooter's chest. No wheezing. "Sounds clear. Let's go to the forest. I'm dying for you to meet Cady."

"Me too?" Gracie asks, arms raised for us to pick her up.

"Not this time, Gracie, but I'll carry you upstairs to Dad's studio, okay? You love Daddy!" I plop her on the floor with a circle of her favorite books and panda around her. Then I dash out and make sure the door's closed tight before Dad fully realizes she's under his drafting table. We leave a note on the fridge saying that Scooter and I will be home by dinner.

It's great to see that Scooter's feeling frisky today, and I lope along after him. When we get to the fallen log that's the entrance to the forest, he comes to a halt.

"I'm not sure I wanna go in there," he says.

"Oh, come on, you've been here a million times, and Cady's anxious to meet you." She isn't, I'm pretty sure of that.

Scooter parks on the log, feet on the house side rather than the forest side. "Be honest, Hannah. There isn't really a girl who lives in the forest, right?"

"There is! You'll see. She said she has lots of friends there, too. Maybe one of them's a guy around your age." Of course, she did say all girls, but Scooter doesn't need to know that right now.

He slowly slides one leg over, then the other, and I do a handspring across the log. That's how eager I am to see what Cady's up to today. We zigzag through the trees, crunching pine needles and leaves under our shoes. Insects scatter, out-racing us. We try not to step on them, or on the lovely white wild flowers that have sprung up since I was here last.

At the clearing, Scooter spots the glistening Moonlight Lake and hangs back. "We're not supposed to go there," he says. He's way more timid since his last asthma attack.

"I've been in it. You've got nothing to worry about. We won't go too close to the muddy banks, I promise."

Scooter's steps are tentative, but he follows me. There are two gently sloping tree stumps close together, and that's where we sit . . . and wait . . . and wait. My stomach's growling, and the two peaches I was planning to give Cady smell so sweet. We slurp them, juice dripping down our wrists, and wait . . . and wait.

"Cay-dee!" I call, using both sticky hands as a mega-phone. "I'm here, Scooter, too. Come on out, Cady."

A tiny ruby-throated bird peers down at us from her nest, as if she's saying, *quiet, my babies are sleeping.*

After ten minutes Scooter jumps up. "Okay, I get the joke. Let's go home."

"We can't! She's here, I swear." I drop the bag, and out tumble peach pits with fruit clinging to them. We watch a giant cloud of insects stampede toward the treasure, which is already swarmed by red ants, and when we look up, Cady is standing in front of us.

"Whoa!" Scooter cries. His eyes are as wide as cucumber slices.

"Do you always have to just pop up like that?" I don't bother to hide my annoyance.

"You didn't hear me because my footsteps are feathery soft." In fact, her feet are bare, and I wonder how she can walk across the rough, prickly forest floor that way. It sure tore up my feet.

As I expected, she's wearing a sundress, like me, and her hair is dyed a freaky black and is now so straight that she must have ironed it to get it to hang that way. It's a fake imitation of my hair, but about twelve shades darker and twice as straight.

"What did you do to your hair?"

It clinks when she flips it off her neck. "Yours is so pretty, I wanted mine to be just the same. I guess I went a little overboard on the dye."

"I can't believe your mother let you do that."

Cady tilts her head and the hair, like a sheet of black metal, flops in one piece to her shoulder. "We're free spirits, women who make history." She squints at Scooter. "You're the pesty little brother that Hannah told me about with the so-called allergies."

Scooter shoots me a look of betrayal.

"I never said he was a pest. He's the best thing in my whole family."

"Whatever." As if to say, *Yeah, right, but I'll let it pass.*

How could Cady be so insensitive? Scooter shuts down. He never fights back except to get a snide zinger in now and then.

"We're going home. Come on, Hannah."

"You just got here!" Cady's eyes cloud over, and her mouth turns down.

I'm a sucker for a sad face. "Just a little while," I murmur.

"Yes!" Her whole face switches, just like *that*. She breaks off a clump of some weedy green leaves with droopy red flowers nesting in them. "Amaranth," she says, "also called pigweed. Here, smell." She waves it under Scooter's nose.

He recoils. "I don't smell a thing."

"That's because your nose is always stuffed up," Cady points out.

"You feeling okay, Scooter?" Me, the worrywart. No wheezing, though.

"Sure." His eyes flash, *get me out of here.*

Folding her legs like a baby deer, Cady drops to the ground in front of us, her dress ballooning around her. "Know what amaranth means? It's from a Greek word meaning immortal. Isn't that a nice thought?"

Scooter is so not up for a language lesson or Greek or living forever. Cady studies his red eyes, his twitching nose. He sneezes five times in a row like a fast drumbeat, wiping his nose on the shoulder of his T-shirt until I hand him a tissue.

"Ooh, are you allergic to pigweed? So sorry." Cady tosses the clump of green leaves behind her, and the amaranth petals scatter to the wind. "So, listen, while we're talking about plants —"

"We're not," Scooter snaps, with his elbows on his knees and his head in his hands.

She ignores him. "You'll never guess what I know about your house."

Scooter says, all nasally, "You must be the world's authority on everything."

"Most things," Cady says with a snicker. "So, if you're wondering why your house is called Nightshade, I have the answer."

"We have to go home right now," I tell her, poking Scooter.

But he looks at Cady with those red-rimmed eyes and says, "What's the story?"

Our shoulders clunk against a fat tree trunk. How easily she did that — pulling both of us into her web.

CHAPTER FOURTEEN

"LONG AGO A WOMAN NAMED VIVIENNE LIVED IN your house," Cady begins, her voice creamy, her eyes looking into the distance. It sounds like a story she's told lots of times before, all flowery words and pictures she sketches in our minds, like poetry.

"Vivienne's hair was the color of sunrise, a glimmering light blond with golden wisps, and it fell down her back nearly to her slim waist. She held it out of her eyes with bright silk scarves of every color of the rainbow. Her green eyes set off a nose as regal as a queen's. Her fingers were long and delicate, made for holding a fine brush."

I ask, "Was she an artist? A painter?"

"Of course she was," Cady says, as though I've offended her with the question. "The house you're living in was built for her in 1895 by her husband, Anthony, who loved her more dearly than he loved his own life. True love is like that, I suppose." Cady locks eyes with each of us. Scooter looks away, breathing okay. I can only whisper, "Yes."

"She named the house Autumn Splendor because of the radiant reds and oranges and golds of the trees. Autumn Splendor was Vivienne's dream house. She was in love with color. When everyone else walked around the village in drab grays and blacks to their ankles, Vivienne wore wild hues of cranberry and lime and persimmon and eggplant."

"She dressed in fruit and veggies?" Scooter snorts. His breathing is heavy and slow.

"She means their colors," I explain when Cady gives Scooter an eye-roll.

"And crimson and cerise, ten different shades of red," Cady continues. "Oh, people laughed at her, thought she was mad. Crazy mad, not angry mad. But, you see, she was an artist, way back when people seldom recognized women as great painters. Her studio was on the third floor of the house."

"Like Dad's architecture studio," Scooter volunteers, sniffling. I hand him another tissue; I always have a supply ready for him.

"Yes, that third-floor room has incredible morning light that floods it from windows on three sides."

How does Cady know such details about our house?

"Vivienne's whole life was painting. Everything, everyone else was a distraction."

"No kids?" Scooter asks. He can't imagine a family without children.

"There were three."

"What were their names?" I ask.

"Lost to history. The children meant nothing to Vivienne. The three of them, two girls and a boy, lived under the tyrannical rule of a governess named Hypatia. Anyway, it doesn't matter because this story is about the mother, not the children. What do you think is the cruelest thing that could have happened to Vivienne?"

Scooter offers, "She fell out one of those windows and cracked her noggin?"

Cady shakes *her* noggin.

"People hated her paintings, and she cut them all up?" I suggest.

"Wrong again."

I have another idea: "Anthony, who loved her so much, fell in love with another woman, maybe that governess person. Aren't there a lot of old stories like that?"

Cady squares her shoulders in surprise. "That would never in a thousand years happen. Hypatia looked like a giant toad."

Scooter sniffles. "Then what did happen?"

"If you quit that constant sniffling I'll tell you." Cady pulls her knees up to her chin, smooths the dress around her, and sinks her chin into the space between her knees. "One night in autumn, the season that Vivienne loved best, a torrential tempest blew in. You might think the storm was terrifying. You might huddle under blankets, or even under your bed, until it tamed and passed. But not Vivienne. She loved the infinite colors of wavy leaves, the blue-black sky, the silver wind and rain."

"You can't see colors of wind and rain," Scooter scoffs.

"Vivienne could. She rushed outside to that small balcony in her studio. Next to your room?" she asks, eyes fixed on my face. "I thought so. Vivienne stood there with her arms raised, to embrace the storm like a lightning rod. She watched a bolt of lightning slice the night sky. That was the end for her."

"Oh my God, she was struck by lightning and died right there on our balcony?" I said.

"Worse," Cady whispered. "From that moment on, she was blind."

"Totally?"

"Yes, Hannah, all color gone from her eyes. It was 1897, people didn't know about diseases that could turn a person suddenly blind. She was convinced that the jolt of lightning burned the vision out of her eyes, though the lightning never touched her."

Cady let that thought wash over us; we didn't say another word.

"Can you imagine the drama, the horror? How she screeched and keened and bellowed and wept? The whole household did, even Bascom, the Maltese puppy. And think of the bitterness that poisoned the house afterward." Tears slid down Cady's cheek, as if she'd been there, as if she were reliving a terrible time in her own life. She dabs at her tears with the tissue I hand her. I kind of sniffle myself. Crying is contagious.

She squeezes her eyes shut, then opens them with determination to finish her story in a flat monotone. "That night Autumn Splendor became Nightshade, for Vivienne only knew dark and shadow, and for her, it was eternally midnight."

I'm charmed by Cady's story. Vivienne is totally real to me, as if I actually knew her in the 1890s, which of course is impossible. Long shadows have fallen on the forest floor. How long have we been here? Hours!

We're both on our feet, reeling from Cady's story. "Come on, Scooter, Mom's going to skin us alive."

"When are you coming back?" Cady asks frantically. "Come on Tuesday, my favorite day of the week. We can spend the whole day together." She doesn't mention Scooter.

"Why is Tuesday your favorite day?" he asks.

"Remember that poem? 'Monday's child is fair of face, Tuesday's child is full of grace.' You'll come at sunrise?"

"Maybe not so early. It's summer, sleep-in time," I remind her.

She lunges toward me for an awkward hug, and it's not like hugging Luisa or Sara, though I can't quite figure out why.

Walking home, that weird old poem kept running through my head. "Monday's child is fair of face, Tuesday's child is full of grace." What's Wednesday's child? And then it hits me: "Wednesday's child is full of woe." Tuesday may be Cady's favorite, but she's definitely Wednesday's child.

CHAPTER FIFTEEN

ONCE WE'RE OUT OF THE FOREST, I REPLAY Vivienne's sad story and our whole afternoon with Cady in my mind. I'm so lost inside my own head and heart that I barely notice Scooter lagging behind me, hanging onto a wagon in the yard, stumbling a few steps, then leaning on the side of the house. His breaths come in short bursts, like the stuttering sound after you've had a big cry. Oh, no! He's doubled over. Again.

"Scooter! Let's get you inside." He pulls the inhaler out of his pocket and tries to suck in the medicine between gasping breaths, three puffs, pause, three more puffs, but it isn't doing what it needs to. I let the kitchen door slam behind us and shout at the top of my lungs: "Mom! Dad! Scooter's real bad!"

Both parents thunder down the stairs, instantly mobilized. You'd think it's a military operation. Phase One: Dad hits speed dial to alert the lung specialist to meet Scooter at the emergency room. Mom tosses her ever-ready bag into the SUV, packed with library books, her cell phone charger, contact numbers, knitting, and Scooter's thick medical file.

She props Scooter up in the back seat with pillows all around him and pulverizes stones in our driveway as she zooms out. She's a pro at this; she can get Scooter to the ER faster than waiting for an ambulance.

Inside, Dad launches Phase Two of the military operation: "Hannah, I gotta pick up Trick at baseball practice. Can you handle Gracie? She's watching a Disney video in my studio. It'll be over in ten. When Franny gets home tell her to start dinner. I'll drop Trick off here, then go to the hospital to help with Scooter. Got all that?"

"Sure, Dad, I'm on it." I'm snuffling back tears — this is the worst I've ever seen Scooter. We could lose him, lose him. No!

Upstairs, Gracie is so wrapped up in her video that she doesn't even notice me. I plant a smooch on her sweet head. She smells like a Dumdum lollipop. Late afternoon shadows cast their gloom over the studio, and I imagine the beautiful Vivienne in this room, more than a hundred years ago, filling canvases with bold brushstrokes of vivid paint — all those vegetable colors and fall colors and ten shades of red.

When Gracie's video ends, she hits the right button to play it again. I can't get onto the balcony, since the door is painted shut, so I sit on the south window ledge with my legs dangling in the air. Mom will go crazy if she sees this. If I spot her SUV coming around the bend on Thornbury Trace, I can slide back onto the window seat inside. She'll be at the hospital for a long time, though, looking after Scooter, so I'm safe.

This studio is where it happened, where Vivienne lost her sight. I close my eyes and cover them with my hands so not a sliver of light leaks in. I spin back inside, and inch my way from one side of the room to the other, trying to imagine what it was like for Vivienne to be struck blind in an instant.

"It's Cady's fault," Scooter says, lying on the family room couch. They kept him at the hospital for two nights until he was stabilized. Mom stayed with him, so I was on Gracie duty and couldn't get back to the forest. This afternoon they released him, and I know Mom will sleep in the twin bed next to Scooter's tonight to make sure he's breathing okay. No one wants to say it out loud, but we all know that Scooter's asthma is getting unmanageable.

"You're saying Cady, like, hexed you? Get real."

"Worse. Up to the time she deliberately waved that flower under my nose, I was just sneezing and my eyes were watering. Garden variety allergies, like I'm used to. But that pigweed in my face really set me off. I Googled amaranth and pigweed. Guess what: it's hyperallergenic. Cady knew it would send me into an attack. She hates me."

"No! She just wanted you to smell the flower."

"Pigweed has no scent. She already knew that. She did it to make me really sick."

"No way, Scooter. That's totally insane."

Gracie's munching an unpeeled carrot. She knees her way up onto the couch, straddles Scooter's stomach, and slams a square board book on his chin. "Read storybook!" she says, spraying small carrot chunks. Scooter tickles her neck and underarms. I love her giggle. She turns to me and says, "Shooter all better!" while bouncing on his belly to emphasize her point.

"He sure is," I reply, though he's really not. Dishes are clattering around in the kitchen where Trick's loading the dishwasher. Scooter, Trick, and I each have two dish nights, but Trick's taking Scooter's shift tonight, and he yells from the kitchen, over the blasting radio, "You owe me big time, dude!" He won't collect. We all look after Scooter, including Gracie.

Could Scooter possibly be right? Did Cady deliberately try to set off his attack? Was she just trying to prove that he was faking it all? I can't believe that. But here I am defending my friend against my brother. "She wouldn't do such a mean thing."

"Yeah, she would. I'm in the way. She wants you all to herself."

Even as I deny it, the truth nags at me.

CHAPTER SIXTEEN

FOR DAYS FRANNY AND I HAVE AVOIDED TALKING about what happened at Food Lion, but the oozing sore isn't going to heal by just slapping a Band-Aid over it. I'm ready to hash it out.

Franny's going through her closet and drawers when I slip into the room and bounce down on her trampoline of an unmade bed piled with clothes.

"Only fifty-nine days until I. AM. OUT. OF. HERE!" she says.

Sheesh, does she have to rub it in?

"My entire wardrobe is so high school. Look at this stuff. Pitiful. I can't take any of it to Athens."

So I start picking through it. I can wear her tops and shoes and some of her dresses if I cut about a foot of fabric off the bottom. This lavender and turquoise tiered skirt will be great with my Navajo shirt. "Mine!" I declare.

"Sure, you just have to roll it up about three turns at the waist." Franny tosses an out-of-shape green turtleneck onto my lap. "Yours, too. I wouldn't be caught dead in this at college."

"Gee, thanks, Franny. Let *me* be caught dead in middle school in this horrendous thing." I stash it under her bed and change the subject. "Looking at this pile of ugly clothes reminds me of something I forgot about because, well, a lot's been going on. Did you know that there's a trunk up in the attic that's full of great-grandma and great-grandpa's stuff? Want to come up with me and see what's inside?"

"Nope."

Well, *that stings.*

She sees me pout and tosses a University of California hoodie at me. "A present for you. I can't wear this at Georgia. It would make me look disloyal."

I breathe in Franny's lemon shampoo scent in the hood. "Can we talk about Cady?"

She spins around. "If you want to."

"She's hard to read. When we're alone, she's really nice. But around you? Around Scooter? She's a different person."

"Overly possessive," Franny murmurs.

"She seems to pop up out of nowhere. She's started dressing just like me. Like she wants to *be* me. She says she used to go to our schools, but I've never seen her. It's like she lives there in the trees or something, and won't tell me where, or what her last name is. She does have lots of friends in the forest, though, and she's promised to introduce me if I swear that I'm a true and honest friend."

Franny shoves a pile onto the floor and sits next to me. "I've heard rumors, something about Moonlight Lake."

"You're saying Cady lives in the lake? Like the Loch Ness Monster? No way!"

"No, I'm not saying that, Hannah. Just . . . there's something odd about that lake and what's on the other side of it."

"That's where her friends live."

Franny gets busy folding sweaters into a neat pile. "Some sisterly advice? Stay away from her friends."

"Why should I? I'm practically a hermit. I've got nobody else to hang out with this summer. I got a postcard from Luisa. She was gushing with news about all the fun she's having with her super-sophisticated camp friends from Atlanta. I guess we're the country bumpkins up here in Dalton." Yesterday, after I read the postcard twice, I crumpled it and sailed it into the yard from Vivienne's studio. Dad's studio.

"To be honest, Hannah, the girl creeps me out."

"She needs me," I reply, almost as a whimper. "Her friends are gone, her whole family's gone, she's all by herself. I don't know how she survives."

"Pathetic," Franny mutters.

Should I tell her what Scooter said? "Scooter doesn't like her, either, and what's strange is that she hates him. Everybody loves Scooter. She thinks he fakes his asthma attacks. And get this, he says she deliberately caused him to have that major attack this week. Is that ridiculous, or what?"

"What did she do?"

"Nothing! Just asked him to smell some flowers."

"Sometimes that's all it takes with Scooter." After a deep sigh, Franny says, "Hey, let's go swimming this week, just girls." Franny offers this vague promise, which I glom on to.

"Tomorrow?"

"Sorry, I work from eleven to seven tomorrow." She's sniffing socks, deciding whether to toss them into a laundry pile or into a give-away bag for Big Brothers/Big Sisters. "Look, Hannah, you're the smartest kid in the family."

"I am?" I ask, all wide-eyed modesty even though I always thought as much.

"You are. You'll know the right thing to do about Cady, but just keep my advice in the back of your mind, okay?"

And then I blurt out the one thing I never meant to tell her. "I don't want you to leave for college!"

She puts her arms around me and holds me close, and I dribble tears into her Rib Shack T-shirt. I'm in deep, so I might as well pour out the rest. "It hurts me every time you give us the daily countdown, like you can't wait to escape from the family. From me."

I feel her chin nod into my hair. "Can I tell you a secret?" she asks.

I pull away to listen.

She reaches for a nickel on her desk and flips it, slapping the Thomas Jefferson side on the back of my hand. "Heads, I can't wait to leave home to start my new independent life."

"Great, just what I wanted to hear."

"But here's the other side of the coin." She tosses the coin again, and it takes three flips for it to land on the Monticello side. "Tails, I'm scared."

Franny? My big sister, scared? "About what?"

She keeps flipping the nickel. "Heads, what if I'm homesick? Tails, what if my roommate smells? Tails again, what if I don't make any new friends? Heads, what if I get in a class that's too hard for me, Shakespeare, maybe, or chemistry, and I have no idea what the professor is talking about? Tails, what if I flunk out?"

And then she's crying into *my* T-shirt. After a long time, when we've both run out of tears, I say, "Do you ever wonder why our house is called Nightshade? I know why. Want to hear a *really* sad story that Cady told me?"

CHAPTER SEVENTEEN

NIGHTSHADE IS EMPTY. EVERYONE'S AT TRICK'S GAME. The old-house sounds that are usually hidden by family bustle now hit me. Floorboards creak and the fridge hums, cycling on and off. The air conditioning drones like a waterfall off in the distance. Curtains flutter in the A/C breeze, and a magnet sown into the hem of a drape clicks against the wall. A tree limb scraping across the living room window sounds like a brush swishing a drumhead. Every sound is amped up, and I'm trembling like an old lady.

Why am I so spooked? What's different about this summer?

Cady.

I wander around Nightshade imagining Vivienne touching walls, counting steps, feeling her way through the house. Upstairs in Dad's studio, I perch on his desk and picture Vivienne standing at the window. She's wearing a long, purple shift, her pinafore apron and tall black shoes splattered with paints of a dozen colors. She's gazing off at the distant mountains, painting what she sees, what she doesn't see with her unfocused eyes swimming in their sockets, desperately searching for vision.

I *feel* her. It's not just imagination. She's here, in the shadows of this room. I'm not the fake Ghost of Nightshade. She's the real one. I jump off the desk, hit the light switch, and flood the studio with brightness. The spooky feeling poofs away so I can think my way through this stuff. It's what I do best, usually.

A car door slams, and my family comes pouring out of the SUV in all its noisy hullabaloo. The circus is back in town, but for a change I'm glad to have them home. I scamper down the stairs to blend into the crowd and hear Mom's worried voice above all the others.

"Scooter, I'm not happy with the way your chest sounds tonight. I want you to take a long shower. Let the steam unclog your lungs, and then it's off to bed. Three pillows tonight. I'll get your meds, and Dad and I will be up to tuck you in."

There's less and less time between Scooter's asthma attacks these days, which scares me. He's had asthma most of his life, but it's never been as bad as it's been this summer. What's different about this summer?

Cady.

In the morning, Scooter's eyes are red-rimmed and he looks skinny and limp. Mom gives him a searching look as she plunks a bowl of Cheerios and sliced strawberries in front of each of us. Dad's already upstairs working in his studio. Vivienne's studio. Gracie manages to get Cheerios in her hair and in one ear, and milk is splattered on the table like paint. Vivienne, the blind painter, would be proud. *Shake it off, Hannah!*

Mom's sitting on a high stool in her Hawaiian muumuu and pink fuzzy slippers, her work uniform, when Gracie spills her whole bowl of Cheerios everywhere.

"Gracie, not again!" Mom cries.

Trick bolts from the table, his practice uniform splattered with milk, Franny grabs her backpack and dashes off to work, and that leaves Scooter and me looking glumly into our soggy cereal while Mom mops up the milk and Gracie caterwauls like a hyena. Typical day at Nightshade. Sara and Luisa would love this.

After breakfast, I'm escaping to my favorite place, the attic, where I can burrow and think about all the peculiar things that have been happening that I have no control over. I like having control.

But first I need supplies. I tug on the jammed kitchen junk drawer. When it finally jerks open, nails and bolts and batteries and wrenches fly all over the kitchen, and I rescue a screwdriver and a lock-pick tool from the pile on the floor, plus a can of oil. Today I'm opening the mysterious heirloom trunk in the attic if it kills me.

The trunk sure doesn't give itself up easily. I'm like a professional safe-cracker, poking away at the lock until finally, success! In fact, the whole lock comes off in my hand, but the trunk has been closed so long that the wood has swollen, and I have to pry it open with the flat blade of a screwdriver. Slivers of warped wood clump on the floor as the top creaks open and I'm smacked with a sharp, chemical smell from white mothballs, like big blobs of hail, scattered inside to protect against insects.

How disappointing! Dad was right — all that's inside is heavy bolts of old cloth. One's flocked with Christmassy colors, another's got blue cornflowers on a yellow background. A third is a Tartan plaid wool flecked with little holes despite the mothballs. I stack a dozen of the bolts into a tower on the floor beside me, and it's a good thing I bothered to take them all out, because underneath the last one is a fragrant cedar lift-out tray, and under *that*, treasure!

In the dancing sunlight, I nearly drop a silver-framed wedding photo sliding out of tissue paper that's yellowed and stiff. Handwritten in pencil on the back of the photo are the words, *Lieutenant Cecil and Moira Flynn, wedding day, August 29, 1945.*

My great-grandparents. The groom, Dad's grandfather, is perched on a high stool behind the bride. Cecil looks dashing in a World War II uniform, narrow-waisted, three gold buttons down the front, a bunch of medals on the shoulder, and a cap low on his forehead. His eyes are unfocused, gazing off to the left as if he wished he were anywhere except in this picture. Maybe he wants to be back on the battlefield, or he's wondering if he has married the right woman.

Oh, but the bride! Moira's white dress is simple, with two rows of seed pearls at the cuffs and hem. A matching veil crowns her dark hair, and pointed white satiny shoes peek out of the bottom of the dress. At her throat is a single string of pearls. White fingerless gloves clutch flowers that look more like a Christmas wreath than a wedding bouquet. She's seated slightly below the groom, her elbow possessively flung across his knee, and the look on her face is pure triumph, as if to say, *I've finally landed this handsome soldier, and I'm not going to let him go.*

I pull the photo to my heart. Cecil and Moira. I never met them. Framed in silver, they're both strangers to me, and at the same time, curiously familiar from another photo in one of our family albums. In that picture they're both old and bent. Cecil leans on a cane, stern and squinting at the flash of the camera. Moira is grinning mischievously, one foot up on a low tree stump. She must have been a real pistol, my great-grandmother!

What else is in the trunk? Here's their wedding wreath, wrapped in a yellowed linen tea towel. The dry flowers crumble as I unwrap them. There's a plate with a gold rim, monogrammed C F M for Cecil and Moira Flynn, with the date of their wedding. And below that, a long, skinny blue velvet box. I open it carefully, and there they are, Moira's wedding pearls. Ooh, there's a note under the pearls. It's creased with age and crackles as I unfold it. It's dated August 29, 1995, their fiftieth anniversary.

As I have occupied the loathsome position of middle child in my family of nine boisterous brothers and sisters, I bequeath these, my wedding pearls, to the middle child of my only grandson, Joseph Flynn. If Joseph's middle child be a boy, then brave little man, my prayer is that these pearls will grace the neck of your bride someday. If Joseph's middle child be a girl, however, praise the Lord for the gift of a strong young woman. My dear, please wear these pearls, whether or not you choose to marry. In either case, they are given with my abiding love.

Your Great-grandmother, Moira

With tears blurring my vision, I hold the pearls to my throat and model them in the reflection of the window. They're a little snug — Moira must have had a doll-sized neck. I snap the clasp and tug to make sure it's fastened.

Something brushes my neck, like cool fingers, sending shivers through me from head to toe. Suddenly the pearls clatter to the floor. I wheel around to see who touched my neck. No one's there, but the pearls were fastened tight, and I didn't just drop them. Someone else did! At least the string's not broken. I squat to pick the necklace up, and that's when I see a slow moving shadow, its hands flat on the rough wood, as if it's feeling its way along the wall.

As a blind person would. And then it vanishes.

CHAPTER EIGHTEEN

SHOULD I TELL CADY ABOUT VIVIENNE'S GHOST? I'M not sure, and first I've got to slam her with the hurtful things she's done to my family. I pinwheel around at a slight noise in the cabin, and there she is. She's done one of her instant-girl appearances, but I'm getting used to them, so I start right in.

"You can't treat my family like you do."

Cady looks puzzled, then gets where I'm coming from. "I know, I'm sorry. I shouldn't have mentioned anything you told me about Franny leaving for college. Forgive me?"

"No! I'm mad! You've said a lot of mean things to Scooter, too, and you triggered his asthma attack. That's unforgivable!"

"Flowers, they were just flowers," she protests. "Anyway, he fakes that allergy thing just to get sympathy."

"Cady! He ended up in the hospital for two days!"

"And he kept you from coming back like you promised."

"*That's* what you take from this conversation?" *Deep breaths. Don't throw pinecones at her!* "You've got a lot to learn about friendship."

Her face is totally elastic, changing expressions in an eye blink. Now she looks as sad as a clown, her hands dragging both cheeks and her lips toward her chin, which mooshes her words. "I don't know what gets into me. I'm crazy-jealous."

Scooter was right. "Jealous of what?"

"People who take you away from me. We're friends. Friends belong together."

"Being friends doesn't mean we own each other. That I can't have other people in my life." I'm trying to simmer down, which is hard because I'm thinking about Sara and Luisa. I know in my heart that they're closer to each other than they are to me. It's like we're not triplets; we're a set of twins and one extra sister. Twinkies come two to a package; we're a package and a half. I know how Cady feels. "Where are your other friends, the honest and true ones you've told me about? We should get together."

Things are clicking in her brain; I see that in her eyes that flit here and there, until she says, "My friends are away for a few weeks, same as Sara and Luisa."

"Okay, but what about your family? They can be friends, too." A busy corner of my brain is saying, *Brothers and sisters don't make up for friends. Siblings are there in the scenery of your life, the JVs, not the varsity team.* But I brush that thought away. Scooter's my best friend in the world. So I ask Cady, "Don't you have brothers and sisters to hang out with?"

"I do. Did. I'm the middle one. The rest are . . . gone."

"You're an orphan!"

"You could say that I'm pretty much on my own."

I'm a total softie, like my dad, and I dissolve into a puddle of sympathy on the rough cabin floor. "You can be part of my family. Come to Nightshade."

She tilts her head, tempted.

"Guess what — there's an official Ghost of Nightshade!"

"What?" Her shoulders snap up and she's blinking like crazy, as if there's an eyelash stuck in one eye.

Everyone likes a good scare, so I lay it on thicker. "Other than Scooter, I haven't told another living soul about this, Cady, and don't think I'm nuts, promise?"

Quick nods, more rapid eye-blinks urging me on.

"The other day I was up in the attic, and I cracked into this old trunk, a family heirloom. Found my great-grandmother's pearls. They're gorgeous, so naturally I had to try them on, who wouldn't? I made sure they were fastened tight. Then something totally spine-chilling happened."

She's listening intently, no more blinkity-blink; her eyes are drilling into mine. It's certainly how I'd feel if she told me her house was haunted. It's like a dream come true.

"I can't explain this: someone touched my neck with cold fingers, and next thing I knew, the pearls went crashing to the floor."

"No!"

"That's not all. Ready for this? I saw a shadow of an actual person sliding slowly across the wall." One more step and I've hooked her: "It could be Vivienne's ghost."

Cady's shaking like Scooter when he has a fever. This is delicious!

"Come home with me, see for yourself. Meet the rest of my family. You already know Scooter and Franny. They'll forgive you. Just don't bring any wild flowers. And Gracie adores you because you gave her M&Ms. You'll like Trick — all my friends have big crushes on him. My parents are great, too. Get this, they have a movie and lunch date every Friday. We're utterly, boringly normal. Come to Nightshade for dinner tonight. You'll see, and then we can hang out up in the attic."

She's stopped shaking. Her shoulders sag and she seems to close up inside them. "I can't."

"Why not?" Now I'm insulted that she's turning down my heartfelt invitation.

"I just can't."

"Tonight? Or ever?"

She looks away, her faded blue eyes unreadable.

"Next weekend, then?"

"Maybe," she says, unconvincingly.

She won't come, I know it now, but why? Is she too jealous? Embarrassed to face Franny and Scooter? Spooked by family love?

Or is she afraid of the Ghost of Nightshade?

CHAPTER NINETEEN

NANA FIONA IS ON OUR DOORSTEP. WE NEVER know when she's going to show up. When she gets the whim, she hops in her 1984 Studebaker, which she bought on eBay, and drives from Poughkeepsie, New York, to Dalton, but she doesn't dare come more than twice a year. More than that, and Mom would go nuts. All of us would, except me.

Nana's a round, top-heavy bundle of super-efficiency on two short, pretzel-stick legs that end in neon-green high-top sneakers. Scooter says she looks like Humpty Dumpty's mother. Actually, she's Dad's mother.

Mom opens the door. "Fiona! Great to see you, and you're right on time, because look at this mess." Mom's arm sweeps around the chaos of our front hall — toys littering the floor, jackets flung in a heap over a bench, an enormous red cooler gaping open with yesterday's picnic. "We're way out of control, as usual." Mom gives Nana a hug, pushes a mug of coffee into her hand, and says, "Work your magic," which is exactly what Nana means to do.

Dad throws his arms around Nana and dances her around the living room a couple of times. "The kids will be thrilled to have you here," he says as he drops her off by the stairs. "Sorry, Mama, deadline looming." Then he disappears upstairs to his studio. Nana's in charge now. Except to provide necessary transportation, both parents will barely show their faces for the next few days until Nana's back in her Studebaker, pointed north.

The first thing she does is line us kids up oldest to youngest, to inspect us like the drill sergeants you see on TV. She doesn't believe in nicknames, which is fine, since I'm the only one in the family who doesn't have one.

"Frances Elizabeth, pin your hair back from your eyes, child. They're lovely green Irish eyes, but your hair's a widow's veil over 'em." Nana Fiona pulls out a red-flocked velvet headband and tucks it onto Franny's head behind her ears.

"Patrick Sean, I see you're wearing one of those infernal baseball jerseys. Fine, but Braves? At least, at *least*, son, wear the Yankees with pride," and she hands him a vintage Babe Ruth shirt that makes him sputter with thanks.

Nana's smile lands on me (and yes, I'm her favorite). "Hannah Ruth, why, you're taller and more rounded out since I was here at Christmas. I pray you haven't grown up too much for this." She lifts a music box with a revolving Georgia peach out of her shopping bag, gives the key a turn, and it plays "Sweet Georgia Brown."

When she comes to Scooter, her eyes cloud a little. "Scott Thomas, you're too thin, child. It's that vexing breath matter, isn't it? Ay, but you're the bookworm in the house —"

"We call the house Nightshade, Nana Fiona," Trick reminds her.

"I don't doubt it," Nana says, "but I don't have to talk about a house as if it's a living person, now, do I?"

Trick snorts under his breath. Lucky that Nana's hard-of-hearing, except when she wants to hear.

Scooter's got his nose in the book she brought him. "Wow, it's the only one in Rick Riordan's *Heroes of Olympus* series that I haven't read. How did you know?"

"I have a camera in your room."

Gracie fidgets beside Scooter, peering into Nana's huge Trader Joe's shopping bag to see what's in it for her.

"And Baby Grace Eileen. Why, you've stopped sucking your fingers at last!" Which reminds Gracie to pop her first two fingers into her mouth and suck the way Scooter sucks on his inhaler. Nana reaches forward and unplugs the fingers with a loud *slerk* sound. "Here, my darlin', chew on this raspberry licorice twist instead."

Nana stands back and looks us all over, then takes in the cluttered kitchen counter and dishwasher gaping open and a hundred paper scraps magnetized to the fridge and pots crusting on the stove and Gracie's alphabet letters scattered across the floor.

"Well, let's get to work, shall we? I've only got two days, but the good Lord made the world in a mere six, so there's hope here." She issues commands, and we all leap to our tasks to restore order. No wonder I adore this woman!

⚹ ◎ ⚹

Later, Nana Fiona knocks and barges right into my room. She nestles on my bed with her thin legs sticking straight out. "Tell me all about your life, darlin'. Don't spare me a messy detail."

Should I? I tell her how I'm worried about Scooter, who's definitely getting sicker, and about Cady in the forest, how she's saving my miserable summer, sort of. "The thing is, sometimes she's there, and sometimes she's not there, and I never know which it's going to be."

"Tricky, that one."

"And then she does something awful, like giving away secrets and calling Scooter a fake, and I swear I'm *never* going back into that forest, no matter how boring and lonely my summer is."

"Yet you do," Nana Fiona says, and I can only nod miserably.

After a while, with Nana and me holding hands, I say, "I have something to show you." I open my bedside table and take out the pearls wrapped in a white silk scarf. "These were your mother's, weren't they? Her wedding pearls?"

Nana rubs the pearls between her fingers with such tenderness that it almost makes me cry. "Mercy me, where did you ever . . . ?"

"A trunk up in the attic, along with this, your parents' wedding picture, see?"

She takes the framed photo out of my hand and rubs her index finger across her father's face. "Oh, don't be fooled by the uniform. My father, Cecil, was a milquetoast," Nana says with a laugh. Then seeing my confusion, she explains, "A timid man. He was a dear, sweet soul, but entirely under the thumb of my mother." She taps at her mother's face. "This Moira Flynn, she was a vixen if there ever was one. As feisty as a filly at the opening bell." Nana lays the picture down on the bed and holds the pearls up to her neck to model them in the mirror. She sinks into her round self like a balloon losing air. "My mother was my dearest friend. Twenty years, and I've not gotten over losing her."

"She tucked a letter in with the pearls. Did you know she meant for me to have them, even though I hadn't even been born when she wrote the letter? Can I ask you a tough question?"

"I don't have to answer if I don't relish it, now, do I?"

Nana's smile carves big parentheses around her mouth, making me think it might not be so bad to be wrinkly someday.

"Do you believe in ghosts?"

"Ghosts, now there's a perplexing question. The answer is, I'm Irish. That should settle it." She says *Irish* like *Eyerrr-rrish,* rolling every one of those r's.

"That's not an answer."

"Oh, 'tis, because there's a long fierce connection between people and ghostly sprites in Irish folklore. The spirits linger between this life we know, and the next that we don't, because they aren't quite done with the business of their lives — loved ones left behind, anger still brewing like spitfire, frights they've never got past. You see?"

"Sort of, but I'm not sure."

"Did you ever hear of a banshee? 'Tis an eerie being if ever there was one. No? Then let me tell you, darlin', and you'll never forget this. You'll be reminded every time you hear your mother's teapot whistle and wail."

CHAPTER TWENTY

NANA FIONA REACHES ACROSS ME AND TURNS OFF the lamp. She loves atmosphere for her stories. We lie next to each other in the gathering dark, sharing one pillow. We're the same height. My feet are bare; her neon-green sneakers point up toward the ceiling.

"A banshee is a female spirit, a messenger from the world beyond. She's ashen, shadowy, and wraith-like. You know her by her wail, for she weeps and screeches ferociously to warn us living souls that someone dear is about to pass into the next world."

I shudder. "So, she's a kind of ghost messenger?"

"What brings you to ask me about such things, Hannah?"

I don't answer right away, hoping she'll think I've dozed off so I don't have to respond.

She rises up on her elbow and peers down at me.

"When I found the pearls up in the attic, I fastened them tight around my neck, but someone unclasped them, and they fell to the floor."

Nana's eyebrows rise, but she keeps still.

"I think there's a ghost in our attic."

"Do you, now! Well, I'll be. And who might be hauntin' this house, do you think?"

And so I tell her about the house changing from Autumn Splendor to Nightshade and back, the year her parents lived here. And about blind Vivienne.

"Ay," she says.

"Then, you *do* believe in ghosts?"

"Of course not! But to be on the safe side, you never know, do ya, darlin'?"

⊰ ◉ ⊱

Yesterday Nana Fiona inspected the refrigerator and freezer and cleared out things that were too fuzzy or too icebergy. By the time we were all awake this morning, she'd been to the grocery store, had sourdough bread rising, and ingredients lined up for Franny to cook three freezer meals.

Also, she has new jobs for us. Gracie's is to pick out ten toys she doesn't love anymore that she'd like to share, and Scooter's polishing silver that's turned black since Nana was here at Christmas. Trick's on a tottering ladder cleaning bugs out of the light fixtures and changing burned-out bulbs. I have the best job, rearranging the pantry and the linen cabinets. (Order, I love it!) We're a beautiful, fine-tuned orchestra of activity, and Nana, the conductor, is everywhere at once.

As I shift and sort things I'm thinking about banshees wailing. I haven't been to the forest since Nana arrived. Is Cady wondering about me?

Lunch done, and the whole house in clockwork order, Nana gives us the afternoon off. "Hannah, I'd like to visit your attic." She doesn't say it, but I think she wants to see the ghost. Nana comes upstairs with me, huffing and puffing between the second and third floors. "I believe I know how Scott feels, though he's sixty years younger than I am. How does a body get to the attic?"

I show her the pull-down ladder with the narrow, open steps, and the color drains from her face as she gazes up into the black hole of the attic.

"Mercy me. Another time, perhaps."

So Nana doesn't get to meet Vivienne's ghost, if that's really what is up in the attic, because by mid-afternoon she's packed and ready to leave as suddenly as she arrived. Mom and Dad reappear to kiss her good-bye and wish her safe travels and take over again as the adults in charge, more or less.

While Mom is trying to figure out where everything is, since Nana and I rearranged so many things, I slip out of the house and return to the forest. It's the cabin in the woods that I want to explore, with the little chairs and the Smokey Bear poster. If I can sneak back there without Cady knowing, I'll find out more about this mysterious new friend.

In the few days since I last visited, there's a lot more green growth. I have to push aside shrubs and tree branches to get to the cabin, which has some sort of vines climbing up its rough walls.

One thing has changed since the last time I was here. Cady's picnic basket sits on the rickety table that leans toward the dirt floor of the hut, and tempts me. I open one flap of the basket. There are no picnic goodies in it, just a variety of loose gizmos, like our junk drawer in the kitchen. I rummage around inside, sifting through batteries and rubber bands and candles and matches and key chains without keys, until I pull out a bottle of blue nail polish. There's an HF in red on the bottom of this bottle. Franny and I have a deal. We each paint our initials on our bottles of polish so we can claim them. This is *my* blue nail polish that vanished days ago! What else does Cady have of mine in here? I scuttle around inside the picnic basket, but there's nothing else I recognize.

How did she get my nail polish? I can't believe that she snuck into Nightshade, into my room, into my private desk, and took it. If she'd asked me, I'd have loaned it to her. I'd probably have given it to her for keeps. Luisa and Sara and I trade nail polish and sunglasses and earrings all the time. We don't have to sneak things out of one another's houses. No, there's got to be some logical explanation. I mean, stealing isn't what *honest and true* friends do.

CHAPTER TWENTY-ONE

SUDDENLY CADY COMES SWIRLING INTO THE cabin like a whirlwind.

"You always sneak up on me!" Once my heart stops thumping, I stick the nail polish bottle under her nose. "How did you get this?"

At first she gazes at it curiously as though she's never seen it, then says, "Oh, that. It fell out of your pocket the last time you were here."

I don't remember having the bottle in my pocket.

Cady waves long, tapered nails in front of my eyes. "See? I love blue polish just like you do."

"If I wore zebra stripes with purple dots, you'd love that, too?"

"Yes, because we're soul sisters." With a look of pure joy on her face, Cady says, "Welcome to my fort! Isn't this absolutely the best place to hide out when you need to escape from your obnoxious family? No one would find you here. Ever."

I point to the poster of Smokey Bear: *Only you can prevent forest fires.*

"Was there ever a fire here?" I ask, because now I see black char marks on the wood that's so rough you'd get splinters if you even brushed by it. The poster and the silent, deserted faerie cabin are starting to creep me out.

With a hand-sweep of the whole crumbling room, Cady says, "This is my personal fort. No invaders."

"Where is everybody?"

"Everybody? Oh, I guess my friends are staying out of the heat today."

"You said they were gone for a few weeks."

"Maybe longer," she says vaguely.

"Do you go nuts being alone so much? Most people would. It's a funny thing. As far back as I can remember, I've craved time by myself, but after a while it gets so lonely."

"Craved? What does craved mean?" Cady asks.

"Oh, you know, it's like when you've absolutely got to have chocolate or else you'll get very cranky."

"Oh, yeah, I crave chocolate," she says flatly.

"Dark or milk?"

"What?"

"Your favorite kind of chocolate."

She opens her mouth, but no words come out.

"Not counting chocolate, what's your favorite food in the whole world? Mine's raspberry pie. Yours?"

Panic flickers across her face. "Food's a boring subject," she snaps.

"Okay, so tell me something that isn't boring, like what's up with these little chairs?"

"They're old, very old. They're for forest creatures to curl up in."

"What kind of creatures?" I ask, all wobbly voiced, imagining the worst.

Cady picks up the shivers in my voice, and her eyes go soft. "Don't be scared, Hannah. Nothing here would hurt you. Trust me."

Uh-oh. Dad once warned me, "Those are dangerous words. There's something untrustworthy about a person who has to remind you to trust in her."

I desperately want to trust Cady.

A large leather tote bag in the corner is bulging with something. I imagine some wild creature's curled up in there, just waiting to spring to life. Cady reaches in and nothing bites her fingers. Instead, she pulls out a giant ball of orange yarn.

"Guess what I have hidden inside this ball of yarn. Three guesses."

"Um, a tiny blue robin's egg? No? A hawk's tooth? Wait, I know, the eyeball of one of those forest creatures who curl up in your chairs."

"So far off." She begins rolling the yarn backward, like she's reeling in a whopper of a fish. Too slow, so she impatiently tosses the ball against the wall and yanks to unravel it faster, until the floor is covered with orange wool spaghetti, and the dense center of the roll is as small as a tennis ball. What's inside? Suddenly I don't want to see what's in there.

She carefully uncoils the last tight bit of ripply yarn and shows me on the palm of her hand an old-fashioned pin, the kind Nana Fiona would call a cameo brooch. A profile of a face is cut into black stone, surrounded by delicate gold fili-gree. Cady hands the brooch to me. It's ice-cold. I yank my hand away, and it clatters to the floor. She scurries to pick it up and hands it to me again, face down this time.

"It's monogrammed, see?"

The initials are engraved in the gold around the cameo: V.A.S.

"Who's V.A.S.?"

Cady's stare is intense. "Can't you guess?"

I turn the cameo over, warming it in my hands until now it's almost too hot to handle. How could it go from ice burn to heat burn in a minute?

"I introduced you to her, the artist? The blind artist?"

My mind flashes to the attic, the pearls, the shadow along the wall. "You mean Vivienne?"

"Yes, V for Vivienne," Cady says quietly. "I knew . . . know her better than anyone. She was my mother."

CHAPTER TWENTY-TWO

"SHE COULDN'T HAVE BEEN YOUR MOTHER! Vivienne lived in the 1890s."

Cady shrugs. "A problem only if time ripples along a straight path, like a clothesline from your window to the magnolia tree in the yard. But what if time is like this orange wool at our feet, coiled and tangled and tossed every which way? Would you believe it then?"

"Absolutely not. It's another one of your juicy stories." *Or lies?* "Here's what I know for sure. Twelve years and sixteen days have passed since I was born." I jab the air in a straight line. "See? Not a wiggly zigzag-all-over-the-place line."

"Oh, poor Hannah Flynn. No imagination," she says, clucking like a demented hen. "Why can't you believe me?"

She's so sincere, so sure of herself. A terrifying feeling sweeps through me like the chill of the wind on your back when you step out of a pool. Right this minute, I'm dragged into the kooky way Cady thinks, and I believe anything, everything she tells me.

Her question snaps me out of it. "How is that brother of yours doing?" The way she asks it sounds like, *Is your puppy house-trained yet?*

"He's getting worse. We're really worried. Nana Fiona, my grandmother, was here for a little while, and she's frantic about Scooter."

Cady wedges herself into one of the little-kid chairs, her feet sticking out in front of her with the toenails painted blue. "It's none of my business, Hannah, but aren't you at all suspicious of Scooter?"

"No! He's been to the emergency room twice already this summer, and the last few days he's been lying around on the couch with a humidifier going next to him to help him breathe."

"You don't think he's just being lazy?"

"Listen up, Cady. Now *you* have to believe *me*. Scooter would love to be playing soccer or climbing mountains, but he can't."

"He could if he wanted to."

"Why are you so hateful? What did he ever do to you?"

"I don't hate him. I just suspect that the asthma thing is his way of getting a whole lot of sympathy in your crowded family when everybody else seems to get the attention."

"You don't understand Scooter one bit. Of all of us, he's

the one who least wants attention, especially for being the sick kid."

Cady gives me a cold stare, and my fury pings against my chest.

"Okay, maybe I'm being a little selfish," Cady says, her eyes softening into sort of a guilty look.

"A *little* selfish?"

"I just want us to be best friends. If Scooter gets sicker and sicker, you'll want to hang out with him, and I'll see less of you."

One fat tear drips down her cheek, which rips at my heart. I curl at her feet on the dirt floor, wondering when all those girls she mentioned will show their faces. It takes a lot of patience and forgiveness to be her friend. I'll bet she chased them away with her demands.

Maybe they don't exist at all! Maybe she made them up because she's miserably lonely this summer. I'm not as desperate as she is. At least I don't want to be.

"We're friends," I assure her, patting her knee until she jerks it up abruptly. "I have time for both you and Scooter, I promise."

"Then, come here tonight," she says in a pleading tone. "We'll swim together in Moonlight Lake. By the lambent light of the midnight moon." She's gone poetic on me again, like when she told me the story about Vivienne.

I listen and nod, my eyes closed. I see us in the calm, black water, circling a puddle of bright moonlight . . . the night eyes of forest creatures watching us . . . opossums, bats, flying squirrels on the hunt for food. Night is *their* time. An owl screeching like a banshee's wail . . . My shoulders jump, which Cady sees. Nothing escapes her.

"No need to be frightened, Hannah. I'm an excellent swimmer. I've saved many lives."

My heavy eyelids drift open. "People that were drowning in Moonlight Lake?"

"I would never let that happen," she says, soft as a lullaby. "Trust me."

At those words, my eyes snap wide open. "Not a chance. My parents would never let me come swimming at night. They don't even know I'm here now, in broad daylight."

"Oh, come on, Hannah, they don't have to know. And anyway, you won't get caught. We're free spirits. Remember, you're going to make history. You're a person who will be remembered forever and ever."

What is she *talking* about? And why am I even listening? What would Luisa and Sara think of a weird conversation like this? They'd freak out. My old friends are so ordinary by comparison with Cady. It's like they're on Earth, and Cady just beamed down from Planet Zrgph. To be honest, the adventure and mystery of being with Cady gives me giant goose bumps. She's awesome, powerful. She makes me want to see what life is like on Zrgph. She's a motorboat tugging me behind her. I want to keep slicing through the waves of the wake of her boat and never stop.

Whoa! *Get a grip.* My conscience whispers in my ear, *Cut the line. Shake off the skis and tread water to the shore. Right now.* Both feelings are equally overwhelming. What's that Newton thing we learned in science last year? Something about all forces come in pairs — equal and opposite reactions. Boy, am I ever having 'em!

Cady has her gaze fixed on me, watching my tomato-red face. I put my fingers to my neck to quiet the throbbing pulse in my throat. Warm fingers, not like the icy ones in the attic. Smokey Bear is staring at me from his post on the wall. They won't let go; neither of them will. It's up to me to break free!

A deep, shuddery sigh pulls me out of whatever power Cady has me locked in. Jumping to my feet, I grab the end of the unraveled yarn and furiously begin rewinding it. Now it's the size of a grapefruit. Now a head of lettuce. Now an orange beach ball, which I jam into the leather tote bag, and I run out the door.

"You forgot something, Hannah." Cady follows me with her hand locked tight. One by one she opens her fingers to reveal Vivienne's cameo brooch. "This could be yours," Cady says sweetly, "if you come swimming tonight. Moonlight Lake invites you, Hannah. Midnight."

Now she's totally creeping me out! I run outside, retracing my steps back toward the place where I sat cooling my feet in the lake and where I waded in to my armpits. Was it only days ago? Seems like months. I feel like I've known Cady all my life — and like I don't know her at all.

I keep running toward the edge of the forest. Is she following me with her silent footsteps? A quick glance back, and there's Cady growing smaller and smaller, standing at the door of the hut with her arms extended toward me. Her words echo in my head:

"Come . . . come swimming. Moonlight Lake invites you. Midnight . . ."

CHAPTER TWENTY-THREE

THERE IS SO MUCH TO THINK ABOUT. I FLY PAST THE rest of the family and scamper up the ladder to my attic lair and lean against the empty trunk. Late afternoon shadows cloud the attic and swim around the walls. There's a *presence* here of something not quite human. I feel it in a warm breath that drifts past me and in a thickening of the air around me. There's not a sound, but I know she's here. Vivienne. If not Vivienne, could it be the ghost of Great-grandmother Moira?

All this has something to do with Cady, though she couldn't possibly have known either Vivienne or my great-grandparents. What's the connection?

Cecil and Moira owned this house for a year, but that was nearly half a century after Vivienne died. No connection. Vivienne lived about a hundred and twenty years ago, in the 1890s. Cady is living now, in the twenty-first century. No connection.

I'm a logical person. Hey, I'm the one who figured out that the smoky, pungent smell at school was three hundred grilled cheese sandwiches on fire. So the reasonable conclusion is that Cady must have gotten the years wrong, or I heard it wrong, or she's insane, or she's lying to scare me, or what she really means is that Vivienne is the generic mother of us all, or Cady's hoodwinking me for fun as I do to Scooter sometimes. Lots of possibilities, all of them too outrageous to make even a shred of sense. I'm not sure what to think about any of this. Only that there's no way I'm sneaking out of the house to meet Cady tonight.

I picked up a letter from my *normal* friend, Sara:

> Dear Hannah,
> London is awesome! There really is a London Bridge, and guess what — it's not falling down! Yesterday we did the Tower of London. The Crown Jewels were gorgeous! And there are these ravens that hang around the tower all the time. They say that if the ravens ever fly away, the whole British Empire will collapse.

That's a lot of responsibility for a bunch of birds. Sara's letter goes on for three pages of London this, that, and everything else, until I swear, I'm never going there even if every other city on earth drops into the ocean. At the end of the letter, she says,

Ta-ta, chum! Oh, how's your summer going?

Thanks for asking, Sara. Finally.

But I guess it'll be nice to have her and Luisa home next week. It'll be the three of us again, like it's always been. Except one thing that's changed: Cady.

That's what I'm thinking about as I make my way back through the forest later that afternoon. Cady and I are sitting on the bank of Moonlight Lake, wriggling our feet around in the water to the rhythm of birdsong. There aren't any ravens, but it's a perfect summery day — not too hot, not too humid — and Cady is acting like a normal person, like my other friends, for a change. She reminds me of a poem by another one of those dead white guys, Longfellow. It goes, "When she was good/She was very, very good,/And when she was bad she was horrid."

So I warn her, "Sara and Luisa will be home in a few days. And here's the thing. When I bring them here, you have to promise you won't be mean to them like you were to Scooter."

"The *sick kid*," she says with a smirk, which I let pass.

"Or the kind of thing you did to Franny, betraying

secrets. And you can't say wild and crazy things, because it'll freak Sara and Luisa out."

"Like what?" she asks, sliding into the water to capture a dragonfly in her cupped hands.

"Like saying Vivienne was your mother, or that you hung out together a hundred and twenty years ago. In fact, don't talk about Vivienne at all." A shiver runs through me at the mention of her name, because I'm convinced that she's the ghost haunting my attic.

"Any other rules?" Cady snarls, releasing the dragonfly that takes off like a jet.

"Yeah, don't talk about time ripples. I mean, you *are* a little over-the-top dramatic."

She splashes toward me and rises out of the water. "Those girls sound like geeks. You have such boring friends."

"At least I have some," I retort hotly. "Where are the friends you're always bragging about?"

"I told you, they're shy. They'll only show up for people who are honest and true friends."

"Haven't I been honest and true?"

"You won't come swimming with me at midnight."

"Yeah, about that . . . I can't do it."

She shrugs her shoulders, as if to say, *it's your dumb choice.*

"I just want all of us to be friends, you and me and Sara and Luisa."

Cady turns toward me with a broad smile that makes her

face shiny, almost transparent in the sunlight. "Okay, I'll be on my best behavior. You'll be so proud of me, I promise."

That's the *very, very good* side that convinces me that Sara and Luisa are going to be as captivated by Cady as I am. Because Cady may be strange, but she's the most interesting thing around for miles. Of course, she sure didn't fool Franny or Scooter.

"Come on," she says. "I want to show you my most favorite thing in the forest."

I dust dirt off my shorts, and let Cady lead me toward a bush that is as tall as I am. Heavy purple berries, blue-black and as sparkly as pearls, hang heavy from its vibrant green leaves.

"Oh! It's so beautiful, Cady. I see why you like it."

"It's called belladonna. That's Italian for *pretty lady*. Isn't that a lovely name? In olden days ladies used it to make their cheeks rosy and their eyes glisten like stars."

"Those fat berries look delicious. There are enough here to make a whole pie. I'll bet they're as yummy as raspberries."

"Sweeter." Cady pops one into her mouth and tosses another shiny berry to a squirrel. His bushy tail flaps in joy as he plucks it up between his paws and waits for more. You'd think he'd scamper away, scared of us, but Cady seems to charm forest animals. Wish I had that knack.

I snap one of those plump berries off the bush. It's firm;

the juice inside is eager to burst. I hold the berry to my lips when Cady stumbles on a root sticking out of the forest floor, knocking me backward against a tree. The berry flies out of my hand and is captured by the squirrel, who skitters away with it.

I reach for another one, but Cady places herself between the belladonna plant and me.

"Not for you," she says firmly.

"Why not? There's plenty to share," and I reach around her.

She shoves my hand away. "There's something I didn't tell you about belladonna. A long time ago, they used to smear the juice of these berries on arrowheads."

"So?" I ask, my mouth still watering.

"And they say that witches use the juice of these berries to help them fly."

"That's the dumbest thing I've ever heard, like those bumper stickers, MY OTHER CAR'S A BROOM."

"Something else. Kings have killed off enemy armies . . ."

"There you go again, Cady. See, that's the sort of drama-queen stuff I don't want you to say in front of my friends."

"You're missing the point, Hannah."

Cady's typical intense stare drills into me. This is the *when she was bad she was horrid* part of her. "The tantalizing belladonna has other names. Devil's Berries is one, but the most common is Deadly Nightshade. Because it's poisonous."

CHAPTER TWENTY-FOUR

I DON'T BELIEVE A WORD OF IT. THAT BEAUTIFUL plant, poisonous? *No way,* I think as I make my way back to the house.

In the family room, the TV is tuned to a game show. Mom, allowing daytime TV? Scooter must be sicker than I think. He's propped up on the couch. An oscillating fan waves back and forth at full blast, along with the air conditioner. Feels like a meat locker in here. A dehumidifier hisses next to Scooter to loosen the congestion in his chest, and oxygen is piped into him through two little nose buds. Between the roaring machines and the obnoxious wrong answer buzzer on TV, it's impossible to talk. Besides, his heavy meds make him drowsy, and he just dropped off to sleep in the middle of a sentence. So I grab my iPad and climb up to the attic.

The word *belladonna* keeps zinging around in my head. Poisonous? I'm thinking of the day Scooter met Cady, how he got so sick that he ended up in the emergency room. Afterward he said, "She did something to me to make me sick," and I teased him for coming up with such a crazy idea. Maybe it wasn't the pigweed under his nose at all. Maybe Cady slipped him some poisonous berries when I wasn't looking? She keeps trying to convince me that Scooter's faking. Is she covering up something awful she did to him?

In a fury, I'm Googling *belladonna poison*.

It's true! The leaves and berries are real toxic. Some animals aren't sensitive to the poison, but humans are. Just two berries could kill a child!

Leaping down the narrow ladder and rumbling down three flights of stairs in, like, twelve seconds, I'm back in the family room where Scooter's camped out. His bony shoulders rise and fall, and his eyelids are so transparent that I can see his eyeballs jumping around inside. Turning off the roaring dehumidifier wakes him up.

"Hey, what are you doing?" he shouts.

"Think, Scooter. That day when I took you to the forest to meet Cady, you got really sick, remember?"

"I get really sick a lot," he says, his eyes so sunken that I want to hug him and wrap the Star Wars sheet around him and let him sleep. But I have to keep him alert.

"You've got to remember details about that day. You told me Cady did something to make you sick. Besides the pigweed in your face, did she give you anything to eat when I wasn't looking? Like something that looked like blueberries, only real shiny and fatter and blacker?"

"Nope." Scooter hunches his knees up so I can squeeze onto the end of the couch. "But that doesn't mean the girl's not evil."

"Franny didn't like her, either. She's a little peculiar, I admit it, but that's what I like best about her. She's sure not boring."

"So what's up with the fat black blueberries?"

"A kid could croak from chewing just two of them. Don't worry, there's an antidote, if you're fast enough. You drink a cup of warm vinegar to cut the effects."

"I'd rather die of the berries."

He means it as a joke, I know, but hearing those words, I get super-scared, scared that we're going to lose Scooter. Suddenly I can't look at him. I flip the dehumidifier on again and mumble something about needing to wash my hair.

Rounding the corner on the second-floor landing, I hear Dad and Mom in her office. Her door's open just enough that their voices carry clearly.

"I don't want us to do it, either, Sally, but maybe we have to consider it seriously."

Mom's voice is firm. "The kids have lived here in Dalton all their lives, and now that we're settled into Nightshade, they've got their own rooms. It's a family home that will suit us at least until Gracie goes off to college. You've got your studio, all that fantastic light, and I've got my office with the mountain view. We've got a great kitchen and plenty of yard. It's everything we need in a house. Everything."

"All true, honey," Dad says, his voice cracking.

They're talking about moving!

"When you left Poughkeepsie to come back here to UGA for architecture, Joe, you never looked back. Our roots are deep in Georgia soil, at least until your mother defected and married a Yankee. But I grew up in Georgia, Joe. The kids should, too."

Not just moving away from Nightshade, but from Georgia. No! Do I push the door open and let them know I am fire-breathing mad about this? Summed up in twenty-five words or less, never! I keep spying on their conversation.

"Your work and mine, it's portable. We can do it any-where. We don't need to be in Georgia, or anywhere on the eastern seaboard," Dad says. "Arizona or New Mexico, maybe. The desert would be better for Scooter than the soupy air we breathe here."

"Don't say that, Joe! Look, Franny will be at UGA in the fall. We need to be here so we don't have to pay out-of-state tuition."

"It's not about money, Sal. Think about what's at risk here."

Their chairs scrape as they get up and move toward each other. Mom's words are muffled in Dad's shoulder:

"I know it, Joe. It's Scooter we have to think about."

"Yes, it's Scooter," Dad says.

Up in the attic, I bury my face in my pillow and cry my heart out. I can't leave Dalton. How could they even consider doing such a thing to Franny and Trick and Gracie and me? This is where my friends are, where my whole life is. When were they planning to drop this horrible news on us? After my heart's already broken when Franny goes off to college? Just before Trick starts high school and has to miss his big chance to play JV baseball for the Catamounts? When Sara and Luisa go off to seventh grade without me, and I end up a lost sheep in some new school in New Mexico? Is New Mexico even in the U.S?

And what about Cady? I'm just getting to know her, which isn't easy. She'll miss me as much as I'll miss her. I'm not moving, that's final. I'll live with Cady in the woods, or with Sara; she's always wanted a sister. Or I'll room with Franny in Athens. I'm sure she'll love having her little sister in her college dorm room. I know, maybe the new family who moves into Nightshade will let me rent my old room from them so I can get to the attic and learn more about the ghost of Vivienne.

I am not leaving here, no matter what Mom and Dad decide.

It's Scooter we have to think about, they said. How could I let them take Scooter away while I stay here? What am I going to do? I'd die without him around, I'd just die!

And then a strange thought pushes the misery out of my mind. Cady ate the belladonna berries, and she survived. Or maybe the poison doesn't kick in for a few days?

I've got to get back to the forest first thing tomorrow to make sure she's still alive!

CHAPTER TWENTY-FIVE

"CADY? CADY!" I SHOUT, FRANTICALLY RUNNING around the bank of the lake the next morning. "Where are you? Please, please come out!"

I force my way through the jungle of greenery; it grows thicker and wilder every day, but I'm careful not to brush against belladonna. Can it poison you just by touch?

At the cabin, I yell, "Cady? Are you in there?" My heart pounds. What if she's on the floor and breathing about as much as Smokey Bear is on the poster? In other words, dead.

I peek in the empty square where the window would be. No sign of her, but maybe she's behind something I can't see from this angle. I inch the door open, ready for the most horrible sight possible.

Everything looks the same as usual, down to Cady's picnic basket sitting on the rickety table that's missing a leg, and the giant ball of orange wool poking out of the leather bag. The black cameo that Cady had buried deep in the wool sits on the table. It's as frosty as sleet. Does she store it in the freezer? No freezer here. In fact, no electricity. My fingers trace the woman's delicate features carved in black onyx on top of white quartz, or maybe it's ivory. The hairstyle and an old-fashioned hair ornament prove that the lady is from another time. Maybe it *was* Vivienne's. The whole piece is encircled in fancy filigreed gold, like a locket Nana Fiona has. And the cameo lady is wearing a single strand of pearls tight around her throat.

I've never stolen even a stick of gum in my whole life, but suddenly my hand slides across the table as if it's not ruled by my brain or attached to the rest of me. I close my fist around the cameo and slip it into my pocket.

There's a rustling sound outside, like an animal in the brush. My heart speeds up. What kind of animal? I don't want it in here with me. Kicking the door shut is dumb, because whatever is out there can crawl or leap or climb in through the empty window. My body goes clammy. I crouch behind the table, which is also dumb, because it's too small to give me cover. At least I can throw it at anything coming into the cabin.

A face appears in the window, and I gasp. It's not an animal, it's Cady with her hair done up like the woman in the cameo! "Hi!" she says, all merry.

"Oh! You caught me by surprise." As usual.

"I didn't mean to scare you."

Her sort-of apologies never sound sincere. "I'm just so glad to see you here. Sometimes you run away, and I'm never sure if you're coming back."

Slowing my thundering heart, I manage to get a few words out. "I was so worried about you."

"How sweet of you. See? You *are* my honest and true friend. What were you worried about?"

"The belladonna. I Googled it, and you were right about the poison, and then I remembered that you ate some of those berries and I . . ."

"You thought I might be dead?" Cady asks.

"Yes! But I see you're alive and up to your usual tricks. I'm trying to think back . . . maybe you didn't really eat them."

"Maybe I didn't," she agrees. "I have some fabulous plans for us this afternoon, before those *other* girls come back to spoil it all."

I start to say, "They won't," but something makes me keep my mouth zipped. Instead I say, "Tomorrow is my brother Trick's birthday. We're all going to the Rib Shack for dinner, because Franny can get a discount. Why don't you come with us?"

"I don't eat . . ."

"What do you mean, you don't eat?"

"Meat," she quickly adds.

"They must have some veggie options. Beans, coleslaw, fries . . ."

"Some other time," she says evasively. Maybe she's just shy about hanging out with my family after the awful things she's said to Scooter and Franny.

"I have to tell you something terrible, Cady. We're moving out of Nightshade, out of Georgia."

At first she looks perplexed. "Why would your family do such a stupid thing?"

"If we move to a dry, desert climate, Scooter will breathe better."

"It's always about pitiful Scooter," Cady mutters. "I won't let it happen."

"I know, I hate the whole thing myself."

"I mean, I will not allow it!"

"You know a way to stop it?" Maybe she has a bright idea that I haven't dreamed up yet.

Cady's eyes narrow into dark, piercing dots. A clump of her dyed-black hair lies on one shoulder that's hunched up in vengeful rage. She's ready to take on a whole army!

I back away, my knees knocking. "If my family moves, can I stay here with you?"

Her whole posture changes. Her shoulders relax, her eyes light up, and a smile spreads across her pale face. "Of course! We'll swim and go on picnics. I can show you how to catch damsel flies in the palms of your hands. Every day will be one big sleepover."

The sudden switch leaves my head spinning, and I know

I couldn't possibly live here in the forest if my family is gone, but it makes Cady so happy to believe I might, that I don't let on. I give myself over to the afternoon, which zooms by, with Cady teaching me more than I ever wanted to know about the forest. Under a canopy of water lilies, we uncover a nest of ducklings smaller than my fist. Hide-and-seek takes us all over the east side of the forest. The only *safe* is the one wild persimmon tree, which I wouldn't have recognized without Cady telling me because there are no actual bright orange persimmons hanging from it in the summertime.

Sweaty from racing around the trees, we wade into the lake. So what if my dress gets soaked. It just feels good to have my toes squishing the cool mud at the bottom of the shallows. All the yucky thoughts and nagging questions about Cady are shooed away, like the annoying mosquitoes sucking my blood. I'm not worrying about Scooter, or Franny leaving, or us moving. I'm here, now. I've never felt so free, not with my family, and not with my other friends. I'm powerful and bold.

So bold, I say, "I haven't been over to the other side of the lake. Let's wade over there."

"Oh, no, the lake's much too deep in the middle to wade."

"Then, let's go ashore and walk around to the west side. From the cabin we're halfway there already. I'm hot, aren't you? It looks so green and shady over on the other side."

"NO!" she shouts. "NO! NO! NO! You must never, ever go over there!"

Uh-oh, here we go again. "Why not?" I ask, pouting like Gracie does.

Cady slogs out of the water as fast as she can, kicking up mud in her wake. I follow, and her splashing water nearly blinds me.

"You haven't told me why," I shout at her back. "Why can't we go over to the other side?"

She's on the shore now facing me, while I'm still knee-deep in the water, my dress slapped onto my thighs.

"Hannah Flynn, I swear, if you go over there, I will never speak to you again. We can't be friends, ever, do you understand?"

I nod, and she probably thinks I mean it. But all those ugly thoughts seep back into my mind. Scooter's asthma . . . Franny leaving for college . . . our family moving . . . and how furious I am that Cady is always telling me what to do, what *not* to do.

My mind's made up. I am going over to the other side of Moonlight Lake the next time I'm here and Cady's not.

CHAPTER TWENTY-SIX

SOMETHING'S ALIVE IN MY POCKET ON MY WAY home from the forest. It's purring against my hip! I panic for a second — what if it's some forest animal, like a frog, which totally creeps me out? Then I realize, oh, it's just my phone vibrating. Maybe Sara's calling from the royal palace on Princess Kate's cell phone. Wait, I didn't take my phone to the forest. There's only one thing in my pocket, the cameo brooch I stole from Cady's cabin. It chills my hand as I flip it every which way, looking for a hidden watch battery. Nothing unlatches or slides open. Then, why is the thing vibrating like a Mexican jumping bean in the palm of my hand, shooting shivers up my arm?

Did I just see the cameo woman blink her eyes? It's gotta be an optical illusion. Angled in a better light, yes, she blinked! I fling the spooky thing to the ground facedown, bury it under magnolia leaves, and run like crazy.

Three steps from our kitchen door, I have second thoughts and turn back to rescue the cameo. It hangs in my pocket like a stone, silent and still, until I get upstairs and hide it in a shoebox on my closet shelf.

The cameo is going back to Cady the second I get to the cabin in the woods!

Last winter, Granddaddy Mason Oglethorpe, Mom's father, told me, "Hon, y'all prolly noticed that life's what happens when y'all've made other plans." It was Christmas morning, and I'd woken up with chicken pox. Granddaddy's wife — we call her Shug, as in short for Sugar, because she's not technically our grandmother — echoed Granddaddy's words, adding, "Bless your little heart, sweetpie. You just go right ahead and scratch."

And I'm under the umbrella of "itchy other plans" right now, meaning I can't get back to the forest to explore what's beyond the lake, like I promised myself, or to return the creepy cameo.

Mom and Dad are on their way to New Mexico, dragging Scooter and all of his medical equipment along with them, to see if he does better in that high-desert air. I'll bet they'll be looking at houses to buy. They say they're not, but I don't believe it, and even if they find the most fantastic adobe mansion in the whole Southwest, I'll never in a thousand years move into it.

Let's not even talk about the shouting and door-slamming and stomping up the stairs when Mom and Dad announced that we might be moving. Franny, the one who can't wait to leave home, shouted loud enough for people camping way down in Big Canoe to hear, "Y'ALL ARE JUST GOING TO ABANDON ME HERE?!"

Scooter felt so guilty about the move that he wandered around muttering, "It's all my fault. I hate my lungs."

Gracie clung to him, saying, "I wuv your wungs, Shooter!"

All the blubbering and bawling reminds me of the banshees wailing when someone's about to pass into the next world. Leaving Nightshade — leaving Georgia — is a kind of death, so I'll be listening for the banshee wail. No surprise: I'm the maddest of us all. Well, maybe Trick's worse. He hasn't been out of his room in three days except to sneak to the bathroom when no one's looking, and to the kitchen after he's sure we're all asleep. I know, because I followed him last night, and we had a little baloney sand-wich picnic washed down with milk muddied with half a bottle of Hershey's chocolate syrup. Mom would have a fit if she knew.

Our parents asked Granddaddy and Shug to stay with us while they're gone, but Granddaddy says they're the travelin' kind, and they have a Panama Canal cruise lined up and paid. So, Nana Fiona is back. There isn't a lot of the usual mess to clean up, since she didn't even make it back to Poughkeepsie before she was called back. Besides, we're all too grumpy to work.

The house is so quiet. No printer going in Mom's office. No footsteps from Dad's studio. No Scooter machines humming and hissing. The huge house is an empty cave without Scooter. Gracie misses him so much that she's started sucking on anything she grabs — dish towels, a wooden airplane, a hairbrush, or two more fingers than usual jammed into her mouth.

❧ ◎ ❧

"Hannah, darlin', I've been thinking about your attic," Nana Fiona says, waggling her eyebrows. "I'd like to see that attic for myself." She means the ghost. How are we going to get her up those narrow ladder steps?

"Trick! Help!" I shout down the hall.

He plows like a bull into my room, streaming the Braves game on his phone. "Sheesh, is the house on fire?"

"Turn that thing down! Nana and I have a geometry problem for you." I pull down the steep, open ladder that is maybe eighteen inches across, and motion toward Nana, who is at least twice that wide.

Trick's eyes move from the ladder to Nana and back a

time or two, measuring both. "Aw, Nana, why do you have to go up there?"

"My parents' trunk is up in the attic."

"It'd be easier to get the trunk down than you up," Trick reasons.

"People have climbed Mt. Everest, where there's not enough oxygen for a fly to breathe. If they can do that, I can do this. If you can't engineer the climb, Patrick, I'll just do it myself," Nana huffs, with her neon-green sneaker on the first rung of the ladder.

Trick gets behind her to squeeze Nana's hips into a package the width of the ladder. This makes her about four inches taller. She's wedged in there nice and tight. One knee comes up to step on the next rung, but she hasn't got a lot of strength in her pretzel-stick legs, so I push her rump up like we do when Gracie's trying to climb up on Mom and Dad's four-poster bed.

Trick swings onto the ladder above Nana's head and grabs her arms. "You push, Hannah, and I'll pull."

"Don't go disconnecting my shoulders, boy. I need them attached to the rest of me, or I won't be able to drive you to your baseball game tonight."

"We're doing the best we can, Nana," Trick mutters, gentler now because she's said the magic B word.

It takes a good fifteen minutes, but finally Nana flops

onto the floor of the attic like a hooked fish, a big one, and she says, "Well! That wasn't so hard, was it?"

"Nah," Trick says, escaping super-fast. I'm already worried about how I'm going to get Nana down. That's for later. Right now we're hoping Vivienne's ghost will make it worth the climb to her attic.

CHAPTER TWENTY-SEVEN

NANA LIES PANTING ON MY ATTIC PILLOWS. "WHAT do we do, call her name?"

"I've never called her; she just comes. If she wants to."

"How long do we wait? Grace will be bellowing from the wilds of her crib any minute. That child's nearly three. She shouldn't be caged in a crib. While your parents are gone, I'll train her for her big-girl bed and the potty, too. Vi-vee-ennnnn, Vi-vee-ennnn," Nana croons.

"She might come if we're quiet," I hint. We wait, the only sound is us crunching Cheetos. No Vivienne, no shadows on the wall, no cold fingers.

"Mercy, if she's going to be shy, or stubborn as an old mule, we might as well delve into that trunk," Nana Fiona says. She's quite a sight crawling across the attic floor.

We wipe our Cheetos-orange fingers on an old rag and flip open the lid of the trunk. Nana pulls out bolt after bolt of cloth, muttering, "Why on earth did my daddy save all this stuff?"

"It's vintage. We could sell it for a lot of money on eBay, Nana."

"Look at this!" She unwraps a ball of something covered in fabric with tiny pink roses on it. Inside are a cup and saucer so thin that you can see right through them. "Oh! This lovely Irish bone china was from my mother's collection. She kept a dozen cup and saucer pairs, each one different, in a beautiful glass breakfront."

This set pictures two lovers picnicking in the country, all in pinks and delicate greens. Nana gently sets the cup into the groove in the saucer — and suddenly the cup begins to rock. Nana rears back, the saucer flat on her hand with the cup nearly jumping off. I steady it, and it stays put for a few seconds, then begins rocking again. We both glance at the window — a big wind? But no, the air's so still that you can see flecks of dust just hanging there.

"Vivienne?" I call quietly.

The cup and saucer both spin out of Nana's hands and crash to the floor, and Nana bursts into tears with the shards at her feet. "My mama's beautiful cup . . ."

I slam the trunk shut, but it flies open with such force that one hinge in the back loosens and clatters to the floor.

"I don't think she wants us here," I whisper, kicking the pieces of china into a sad heap under the window.

Scrambling down the ladder is much faster than going up.

Back in my room, Nana catches her breath on my bed. "Tell me, what just happened up there, darlin'?"

All I can do is shake my head.

Nana reaches into the drawer of my bedside table and lifts out the little bundle wrapped in the white silk scarf. "At least that evil spirit — or whatever she is — didn't get my mama's pearls." She wraps them again and sets them back in the drawer. "What's this, something Shug gave you? Looks like her tacky style."

The cameo! "It can't be there," I cry. "I stood on a pile of books to put it in a shoebox way in the back on my closet shelf."

Didn't I?

Nana says, "You're sure?"

"Yes, yes!" I am. I think.

"Hmm," Nana says, "So now we know that Vivienne isn't confined to the attic. She can materialize anywhere in this house."

Like Gracie's *wady* in the broom closet.

Nana's hooded eyes are pulled close together and her forehead is more wrinkly than usual.

"Hey, guys, come down to the family room," Franny shouts from the bottom of the stairs. "Mom and Dad and Scooter are on Skype."

I rescue Gracie from her cell, sling her over my hip, and

run down the stairs with Trick. Nana waddles after us, muttering, "Who decided a house should have so many stinking stairs?"

Scooter's face is the first I see. It's hard to tell on the screen if he looks healthier or not. We all talk at once, like at our dinner table.

"Feeling better, Scooter?" That's me.

"Yeah, I guess," he answers, looking forlorn, as if he feels even guiltier that the air is better for him.

Gracie puts her palm to the screen and says, "Hi, Shooter!"

Mom and Dad poke their heads around Scooter's.

"Mama! Daddy!" Gracie screams.

"Hi, Gracie." Mom looks like she misses us terribly. Believe me, I know what that feels like.

Dad chimes in, "Since a lot of people come out here for the dry air, there are good allergy specialists in Albuquerque."

I don't want to hear *that*. It's just another reason to make us move. What is it Granddaddy says? *Jest another nail in the coffin.*

Dad's still talking. ". . . So we figured we're this far west, might as well keep going another 450 miles to Denver. That's where National Jewish Health is. It's a hospital that specializes in what Scooter's going through."

Trick says, "You're putting my only brother in a hospital way out there in the wilderness?"

"Not *putting him*," Dad says. "They're going to evaluate him and see what the best way is for all of us to deal with his asthma."

I can't wait to tell Cady how wrong she is. Scooter's definitely not faking it if a national allergy hospital is checking him out.

"Are you back there, Fiona? I can't see you," Mom asks.

Nana leans forward and mugs for the camera.

"Is it possible for you to stay with the kids for four more days? We'd be home by the weekend."

"I could move in permanently," Nana teases.

Dad quickly jumps in. "Don't do that, Mother, please!"

"Sure, kids, take what time you need to get Scott on the right track. I should have Gracie potty-trained by then."

Gracie runs to the downstairs bathroom and back with her potty seat, which she slaps against the computer screen.

"Franny? Are you being helpful to Nana Fiona?" Dad asks.

At the same time that Franny says, *not really,* Nana says, *she sure is,* which makes us all laugh.

Scooter takes two puffs on his inhaler. "I wanna go home."

"Come home wite now, Shooter!" Gracie cries, and that's how we all feel.

It'll only be four more days until he's back with us, where he belongs. But in four more days, a lot can happen around here.

CHAPTER TWENTY-EIGHT

"YOU'RE HOME!" SARA AND I HAVE A BIG haven't-seen-you-in-ages hug at my kitchen door. She looks around at the cleared countertops, the sparkling stainless steel oven, the row of matching tea towels in neat folds. "What happened here?"

"Nana Fiona." That's all I need to say.

She nods in understanding. "I have so much to tell you." It's all about London and *the royals,* as if she dropped by Buckingham Palace at four o'clock every afternoon for tea. She has a hint of a fake English accent and peppers her stories with words like *telly* and *fortnight* and *cucumber and watercress sandwiches,* which sound gross, even if that's what they serve at tea time at the palace.

After about ten minutes of *pram* for baby stroller and *lift* instead of elevator, I interrupt her. "I have a lot to tell you, too. Big news. There's a new girl our age in town."

"Get outta here! Nobody new's come since first grade, when that Swedish girl, Freja, was here for a month. Tell me everything, her name, her birthstone, her astrological sign, everything!"

"I'll do better than that. I'll take you to meet Cady. In the forest."

"Her family's moved into the forest behind your house?" Sara asks. "What are they, like, faeries?" Her eyes are dancing with the joke, but I don't know how to answer. And there are more unanswerable questions.

"Is she nice?" Sometimes not. "Last name?" Unknown, maybe unknowable. "Skinny? Chubby? Long hair, short? Perfect skin, like London girls? As upbeat as Luisa? Ooh, Luisa will be home tomorrow. Have you been getting her texts from camp?"

Not a single one in the last two weeks.

"She's having a great time," Sara continues. "So, about Cady. I can't wait to meet her. Not today, though. I've got to return books to the library, which I forgot about before I left. I probably owe my whole summer allowance in overdue fines. Come with me. We can ride our bikes. Then you can tell me more about Cady on the way."

The library is a big, bustling, regional headquarters for the county, with lots of computers, lots of books, and lots of people. Who's the first one we see? Cady herself. How does she show up wherever I go?

She runs right over to us and asks, "Which one are you, Sara or Luisa?"

"I'm Sara, and let me guess, you're Cady, right?"

"World-famous!" She grabs Sara's arm and leads her away from me, as if the two of them have things to whisper about that I'm not supposed to hear. My face burns as I watch them across the room in excited conversation. Sara's face is glowing and they're both laughing as if they've been friends forever. A pang of jealousy zings through me. Cady said *she's* the one who's jealous? I'm worse.

Next thing I know, Cady's at the checkout desk talking to Mrs. Cornish, one of the library assistants, and Sara ambles back to me. Her *old* friend.

"Cady is amazing! So cool. She's hilarious, don't you think? And she adores you. But that hair! Is it a wig?"

"I don't think so, just over-dyed."

Cady's disappeared, so I drag Sara over to the checkout desk and ask Mrs. Cornish, "Cady, that girl you were talking to? Do you know her last name?"

"I have no idea," says Mrs. Cornish.

"Could you please check the computer? You could find it if you sorted by first names."

Mrs. Cornish taps in a few keys, then remembers, "No, Miss Cady doesn't have a library card. She's not in our files."

"Because she's so new in town?" Sara asks.

"Oh, no," Mrs. Cornish says. "She's an avid reader. She just never checks out materials. But she's been coming to the library for as long as I've been here."

"What?" Sara and I exchange looks, and I whisper, "This makes no sense. Nothing about Cady makes sense."

Mrs. Cornish smiles, flashing a gold molar. "I suppose that's why she's so charming."

✧ ◉ ✧

Mr. Mosely's crew is finally here to begin work on the balcony outside Dad's studio. He thinks it'll take five days. Nana Fiona will drive the carpenters and painters bonkers, so I predict they'll be out in a day and a half. The hammering and broken glass and sickening sound of wood winching away from wood sends me running to the forest, though these days, everything seems to. This could be the day I meander over to the other side of the lake if Cady's not around.

But she's watching for me on her side of the fallen log, and when she spots me, she motions for me to hurry over.

Shielding her eyes from the sun, she points toward our house and the truck and equipment feeding into it. "What are they doing at Nightshade?" she demands.

"Fixing the third-floor balcony."

"No! They must not!"

"It's one of the nicest parts of the house, and right now nobody can use it because it's practically falling off the outside wall of my father's studio."

Cady's a total wreck, pacing, wringing her hands, tearing at leaves.

"What's wrong? Why are you so upset about the carpenters?"

Her eyes bullet into me. "Don't let them do it," she pleads.

"Why is it any business of yours? You're not paying for it. And you're not living in that house with the carpenter noise and sawdust or standing under a balcony that could snap right off and make mashed potatoes out of anyone walking by."

Cady backs up into the woods, gasping for breath like Scooter at his worst. "Don't say I didn't warn you," she stammers, then runs between tall pines until I can't see her. The only thing left of her is the surprising scent of candlewax, and I can't help thinking about Smokey Bear. Lighting candles in that small tinderbox cabin — how dangerous is *that*?

CHAPTER TWENTY-NINE

A DAY'S GONE BY AND I'M IRRESISTIBLY DRAWN back to the forest. The cameo is pressing against my hip in my jeans pocket as I follow in Cady's path, but she doesn't know I'm trailing her. She's way ahead of me, almost to her little hut, when she suddenly turns around. Does she know I'm here? I squat behind a live oak to hide behind its generous trunk. She's in the cabin now, and the door's closed. I advance a few feet, then a few more, quiet as snow. I tiptoe up to the cabin, and sneak a peek in the window. A fat yellow candle melts onto the wooden slats of the floor, and its flame dances toward the ceiling with a small plume of smoke. Cady's sitting on the floor, arms wrapped around her belly, and she's rocking and moaning, like she ate too much pizza. Her eyes are closed and her face glows in the candle flame while Smokey Bear smiles down on her.

A stab of guilt pierces my conscience. I'm the caregiving type. I'm the girl that curls up at the end of the couch with Scooter when he's feeling sick. I'm the girl who gets Gracie up from her nap when she's cranky, or just wrestling with a dream she can't tell me about. I'm always *there* for my friends. But something I can't understand says, *Mind your own business, Hannah Flynn. Leave Cady to her grief, no matter what's causing it. This is your chance . . .*

Yes! My chance to steal over to the other side of the lake while Cady's in her own world in the cabin! I lay the cameo on the doorstep, hoping a forest critter doesn't carry it away to his lair as a present for his family. The gold around the onyx profile glimmers in the fading afternoon sun.

The cabin is halfway between *this* side and *that* side of Moonlight Lake. Still, it's a long walk around the lake over bristly groundcover and jutting roots. Frogs in the lake call to one another. You'd think they'd get bored repeating the same syllables over and over. Cicadas fill the air with their singsong, like a zillion insects in concert, stopping and start-ing at exactly the same time. Who's the conductor giving the signal?

I dash from behind one big tree to another for cover. Nothing's going to stop me now, even if Cady's following me. I have to know what's on the other side of the lake.

The low growth is thick; you can barely get a foot between the bushes. I shove one aside with my rear, hearing the crunching of broken branches as I slide through the thorny hedgerow. Beyond it is a large open field with tall grass waving like wheat in the gentle wind. Parting the grass, I keep walking. There's nothing and no one over here. Very curious. I expected to see a circle of houses where Cady's friends live, in a small village with a grocery store and a computer repair shop and an outdoor café, all of it shaded by huge, leafy trees — cottonwoods and magnolias with ancient, knotty trunks.

There's none of that. What I see instead is flat, bare land. Beyond the tall grass is more grass cropped close to the ground, as if it's been grazed by a hundred starving goats and cows, but there's not an animal in sight.

I keep walking, half of me quivering with the excitement of discovery, and the other half aware that I'm farther and farther from home, as though I've stepped through some portal into another world. It's a huge relief to see a plane as small as a crop duster circling overhead. The pilot waves to me and put-putters away. Besides him, there's no sign of life.

Off in the distance, beyond a circle of low, leafy bushes are several short stone outcroppings, reminding me of something mystical like Stonehenge. They're not lined up neatly — no, they're stuck in the ground, facing every which way. Getting closer, my heart starts to pound. Why should these small monuments fill me with such dread? Something's so wrong here. Those stones are menacing because . . . because . . . now I'm close enough to see what they are.

Tombstones.

Some are old markers, pitted, chipped, and crumbling, that look like they've been around since the beginning of time. Then there are some newish shiny, pink marble ones.

This is a cemetery. Trembling, I reach for the nearest gravestone and run my hand over its notched, arc-shaped top. My fingers trace the etched words on the front:

Here in Effigy
Lies Olivia Bainbridge
1996–2008

A girl who only lived twelve years? How sad is that? The next stone is engraved with those same words, *Here in Effigy*, and the names are Clarinda and Cassandra Danbury, 1938–1950. Twins? Both twelve years old, and they died together! My heart bursts in sympathy, but my throat tightens around choked cries as I move on to the next stone. *Here in Effigy Lies Bonnie Ava Amberson 1899–1911*. The math is too familiar; Bonnie Ava was also twelve.

Four girls, all living only twelve years, in different times ranging from 1899 to 2008, one hundred and nine years! Who were these girls? There are more gravestones, but I don't want to know anything else about them. The horror sends me racing back across the stubbled lawn, through the tall grass and the thick bushes, over the bristly, gnarled groundcover, around the lake that's swallowing the sun, past the cabin — and right now I don't care if Cady sees me — past the belladonna, through the pine trees, across the log at the mouth of the forest, and home to Nightshade.

Because now I know that these girls, Olivia and Clarinda and Cassandra and Bonnie Ava are the *friends* Cady wants me to meet.

And they're all dead.

CHAPTER THIRTY

MY BRAIN'S IN A FLURRY OVER WHAT I SAW IN THE forest cemetery, but there's no time to stew anymore because, at home, Nana Fiona is in a snit. The carpenters have raised a blizzard of dust that's snowing down from the third floor, and Gracie has made dust-mud soup on the kitchen floor with apple juice from her sippy cup.

"Where were you, Hannah? It's been bedlam here. Patrick just flounced out of the house, threatening to join the army or the circus, whichever one will take him first. If you ask me, the circus sounds like more fun. Where did you say you were?"

I'm stomping a wad of paper towels around on the floor to soak up Gracie's mess. "No place special." *Just visiting a bunch of dead girls my age.* "Don't worry about Trick. He makes these threats a lot, but always comes home when his stomach starts rumbling."

Gracie smears the floor with the muddy paper towels.

"Mercy, child!" Tossing the soggy mess in the trash,

Nana drops her ample rear onto a padded kitchen chair and sips from a half-gallon pitcher of iced tea. "Ay, I am too old to manage this zoo. I'm not a spring chicken, you know." She rattles her clinking ice cubes. "I'll make it until your folks get home after lunch tomorrow, and then my trusty Studebaker and I will hit the open road."

"I'll miss you, Nana. Is Scooter coming home with Mom and Dad?"

"Scott? Of course, he is. Did you think they were going to leave him out there in the wilds of Colorado?"

It's a big relief that Scooter's coming home. I have an awful lot to tell him as soon as I can spirit him off alone.

Rested, Nana gets up and starts pulling flour and baking powder out of the cupboard and spins toward the fridge for butter and milk.

Franny bursts in like an explosion, her Rib Shack apron smeared with barbecue sauce. "I'm sticky all over, so I'm heading right to the shower. Guess who I picked up on the way up Thornbury."

Peeking out from behind her is Luisa. "I've missed you!" She rushes forward to hug me. She's even browner than usual from her weeks at camp, and her dark hair is sunbleached blond in streaks. "I stopped at Sara's," she says.

Sure she did. She wouldn't even think of seeing me first.

"So Sara already told me about that new girl, Cady." Luisa frowns and plucks three cherries out of the fruit bowl, then doesn't know what to do with the pits, so she pushes them into the dirt around Mom's potted petunia. "Mulch," she explains. "This Cady person sounds kind of weird. Do we like her?"

Sheesh, how do I answer that? "Sometimes yes, sometimes not so much. She's unpredictable. She sure likes Sara, though, did she tell you?" I'm remembering how it stung, no, how it *stunk*, when Cady swooped Sara away in the library, cutting me out of their conversation like I was an invisible toadstool. Maybe that's it — Cady's sometimes invisible! Sweeping the thought aside, I force a tinny laugh. "Cady and Sara are sudden best friends."

Luisa rolls her eyes. "Kind of overkill, you think?"

"Exactly."

"What are you two nattering about?" Nana points a wooden spoon thick with biscuit batter.

"That girl I told you about who lives in the forest, remember?"

"I remember every word you ever uttered," Nana says, beating the spoon against the side of a bowl. She's started bacon sizzling in a cast iron pan, making my stomach growl. I am itching for Nana's biscuits and redeye gravy. Hope there isn't a lot of carpenter dust from the balcony job working its way into the dough.

Gracie towers on a chair next to Nana and gobbles a handful of biscuit dough.

"Grace Eileen! Leave some for the oven."

"Guess what," I whisper to Luisa. "There's something strange going on in our attic."

"Hint?" Luisa asks, and I motion with my eyes and a slight nod of my head that it's not for Nana to hear. Nana knows all about it, of course, but still.

"Gotcha," Luisa says, then rattles on about camp and poison oak — *better than poisonous belladonna* — and sailing and trust walks.

Which gives me an idea. Sara and Luisa need to know Cady better before I tell them about what I saw in the cemetery. Maybe they can help me figure out why Cady thinks she's friends with a bunch of dead girls. "What's up this afternoon?"

"My mom's taking me to the Laundromat with thirty loads of gross camp laundry that smells like pickled sweat. Why, what are we doing otherwise?"

"I'm calling Sara to see if the three of us can take a little *trust walk* in the forest."

Nana raises her eyebrows, but doesn't say anything.

"Yay! I get to meet the mysterious Cady No-name."

"If we can find her. I don't know where she hides out, and she only shows up when she wants to."

Luisa pulls out her cell phone and punches in Sara's

number. In two minutes, it's all set. The pickled sweat will have to wait. We're on our way to the forest, Sara and Luisa and me, just like old times. It'll be three of us against one. They're *my* friends, not Cady's.

She can't take them away from me.

CHAPTER THIRTY-ONE

"WOW, THOSE PLUMP, JUICY BLUEBERRIES LOOK yummy!" Luisa says, plucking a deadly one off the bush.

"No! Don't put it in your mouth," I shout. "Belladonna berries are so poisonous that you wouldn't even know what happened to you before you keeled over dead."

"You're kidding, right?" Sara asks.

"Well, maybe not that fast," comes a calm voice from behind a cottonwood tree.

Sara whirls around and Luisa drops the berry. "Cady?"

"The one and only! And you're the Third Musketeer, Lucy or Lisa or something, right?"

Sara reminds her, "You know her name. At the library you asked me if I was Sara or Luisa, remember?"

"There's so much on my mind that I forget little details."

What could she possibly have on her mind when all she does is appear and disappear?

Just then a cloud sweeps overhead, turning the forest

ceiling into twilight, which makes Luisa fidget with a strand of her sun-bleached hair.

Cady watches intently. "Feeling nervous, Luisa?"

"No, not at all," Luisa lies.

"Are you sure? Sara told me how you're real scared of the dark."

"Sara! You didn't!" Luisa cries, and Sara looks stunned. I'm sure Sara wouldn't have said anything to Cady about it in the short time they were talking at the library, but Cady has an eerie way of knowing everybody's dark secrets. No one knows that Luisa sleeps with a flashlight shining next to her head and backup batteries under her pillow except her family, Sara, and me (and I guess her camp cabin mates now).

"I didn't realize this fear thing was a sensitive issue with you." And as if Cady willed it, the cloud cover lifts, and rays of sun shine down between the tall pines. "Forgive me?"

"Sure," Luisa says grudgingly, because it's hard to stomp on the face of an apology that almost sounds sincere.

"Good. Let's start over and have some fun. Look, I've shoved a flat barge into the lake. We'll pretend it's a fabulous cruise ship sailing us to Montego Bay or the Panama Canal, like Hannah's grandparents."

I'll bet if we took a vote, none of us would want to step foot on that flimsy boat, but somehow we all follow Cady to the bank of the lake where she's got it anchored with heavy rope around a cottonwood tree. It's not even a boat, really. It's just a bunch of planks nailed together. There aren't even sides. It'll sink with the weight of the four of us!

"Is it safe?" Sara asks warily.

"Absolutely. Nobody drowns in Moonlight Lake," Cady promises. "Of course, our friend Hannah doesn't believe that. She won't come swimming with me at midnight. And I know you wouldn't either, Luisa, since it'd be scary-dark. Would you do it, Sara?"

"I don't know. I'm kind of a big chicken."

"I'll do it!" Luisa says, pounding her knees with both fists. "As long as there's moonlight."

"There's a full moon Saturday night," Cady says, her face glowing with excitement. "Who's up for it?"

Sara hesitates. "I guess if Hannah and Luisa are in . . ."

"See, Hannah? Your friends are honest and true *and* brave."

"We'll have to sneak out of the house after everyone's asleep," Luisa says. "Not one single parent in the whole state of Georgia would let their kid go swimming in a lake at midnight. Well, I guess your mother would," Luisa adds, pointing to Cady.

"I'm a free spirit. I do whatever I please."

"Must be nice," Luisa says. "My parents are like the Georgia State Police."

Sara murmurs, "What if your mother does find out, though, Cady?"

"Oh, she's busy with her own stuff. Doesn't pay any attention to me."

Which is so sad. Wait! I thought she told me her parents were dead. In fact, that Vivienne was her mother, and she's *way* dead. I don't know what to believe.

"So, y'all will come Saturday night at midnight? It's *the* best time to swim. The water's calm and cool, and you can float on your back and watch the stars dotting the black sky."

"You said there'd be a full moon," Luisa reminds her nervously.

"There will be. I promise." Cady's voice is dreamy, as if she and the moon share something special that the rest of us do not. "Y'all are coming?"

My knees are shaking, and Luisa's twisting her hair into a snarl. We look from one to the other, each of us embarrassed to say NO, NO, I WON'T GO! So we do one of those things where you pile your hands and make a pledge, like we used to do a pinkie promise when we were little. And then, I swear, Cady reads my mind!

"Okay, girls, it's like a pinkie promise. We have to seal it with a chant, ready? *Luisa, Sara, Hannah, and Cady; midnight moonlight loon nightshady.* Say it with me," she urges.

It feels stupid and embarrassing. It's something kindergartners would do, but we all four chant it together, a solemn pledge that three of us do not want to keep: *Luisa, Sara, Hannah, and Cady; midnight moonlight loon nightshady.*

CHAPTER THIRTY-TWO

AFTER THE CHANT, WE PRETEND WE FORGOT about Cady's boat, because Sara and Luisa and I don't want to hang around one single minute longer. We're all clumsy trying to hug Cady good-bye. She slides out of our hug and dusts herself off as if we've given her a tropical disease, and that's without going to Montego Bay on her hopeless boat. So the three of us start home, silent and grim and really confused.

"Hannah! Wait a minute!" Cady comes running up to me, and we freeze. "You left something." She hands me the cameo. My first reaction is to pull my hand away so it sinks into the bog of the forest floor. I don't. Her gaze is so forceful that I close my hand around the cameo and walk on silently, while Sara and Luisa stare at me in wonder.

When we hear Cady's footsteps growing dimmer behind us, we all blather at once.

"That is one wacko girl," Luisa mutters. "That boat of hers!"

Sara says, "I wouldn't have put one toe on it. It's doomed. It's the *Titanic* of Moonlight Lake."

"So, what did she give you?" asks Luisa, who pries open my tightly locked hand. "Oh, disappointing. It's just some kind of old-fashioned pin."

Sara says, "It's so pretty. Whose is it, Nana Fiona's?"

"No." One quick word that sounds like a door slamming, but only opens up their questions: whose pin, why did Cady have it, why did she make a big production out of giving it to me, and why is my hand shaking as I hold it?

Sara can see that the cameo has me spooked. "Better tell us the story."

My voice quivers. "I'm pretty sure it belongs to Vivienne."

"Who's she?" Luisa asks. "Another one of Cady's tribe of crazies?"

Shaking my head, I blurt it out: "Vivienne is the blind ghost who lives in our attic."

"Ooooh," Luisa says, "The G-g-ghost of N-n-nightshade! Wait, how can you tell if a ghost is blind? She has a ghostly seeing-eye dog?"

"I'm not kidding."

Sara and Luisa both stop suddenly and give me a good, hard glare. I know they're starting to think that I'm as crazy as Cady.

"Let me see that." Luisa reaches for the cameo, but I pull it out of reach. Annoyed, she mutters, "What*ever*."

A few steps ahead of the others, I dare to look closely at the cameo. It's not moving or blinking or freezing my hand or doing anything strange. Maybe when I thought it *was*, it really *wasn't*. Just my overactive imagination, which has been on hyper-alert ever since the first day I met Cady.

I drop the cameo into my pocket.

Dusk is falling. Luisa's getting nervous. "No more talk about ghosts and stuff, okay? This is all too weird. Did they just let Cady out of the loony bin?"

Sara says, "Loony bin, wow. I just put two and two together. She's really into the midnight moonlight thing, and isn't *luna* a word that means moon, as in moon-crazy, as in lunatic?"

"What did we get ourselves into?" Luisa moans.

"We are not going to the lake at midnight, are we, I mean really?" Sara demands. "My mother would have a cow if she knew I was even thinking about it."

"At least our parents care about us. Cady's? Totally out-to-lunch," Luisa says. "I don't know — maybe she's lucky."

Sara says, "I'm sure she tricked us. She does witchy magic or something."

"That's what Scooter thinks."

"Must be true. Otherwise I would never have agreed to do such a stupid thing as swimming at midnight," Luisa says.

She's right. But then why are these words falling out of

my mouth? "We made a pledge. *Luisa, Sara, Hannah, and Cady; midnight moonlight —*"

"Yeah, yeah, we know the rest," Sara mutters.

We trot along at a steady pace, crunching pine needles under our feet.

"I'm sorry about the afraid-of-the-dark thing, Luisa. Honestly, I never said a word to her about it," Sara says.

"I believe you," she says, glaring at me. "So here's my question. Is Cady just mean, or really insensitive, or totally nuts?"

"All of the above," Sara answers.

I don't want to defend Cady, but here I am doing exactly that again. "She *says* she acts crazy because she's jealous of the people I'm close to."

Luisa adds, "She sure doesn't get how friendship works."

I can't help thinking about her "friends" in the cemetery, Cassandra and Bonnie Ava and the others. "I'm sorry," I say. "I shouldn't have brought you here."

Sara says, "And now we've got this midnight moonlight thing to deal with."

"We still have two nights until Saturday," Luisa assures us. "That's plenty of time to think about it and talk about it a few hundred times."

"Until we talk ourselves out of it?" Sara suggests hopefully.

"Before that, there's something else in the woods I have to show you. It's on the other side of Moonlight Lake." We're almost to the mouth of the forest. I swing my legs over the fallen log toward home. "Tomorrow morning, meet me right here at six o'clock. It'll still be cool, which is really good, because what you're going to see, I promise, will set your minds on fire."

CHAPTER THIRTY-THREE

SARA, LUISA, AND I MEET AT THE FALLEN LOG. Sara's slathered on sunblock that's crusting into a white paste on her nose. She smells like heavy-duty insect repellent. Luisa, fresh from the outdoorsy camp, wears a camouflage cap with drop-down shades and a thing that hangs over the back of her neck.

"Sheesh, do ya'll think you're going on safari in a South American jungle?"

Sara says, "I burned to a crisp out here yesterday. I'll totally molt in three days."

"We need every defense possible against Cady," Luisa declares. She looks up at the pink morning sky. "Whose idea was it to come out here at six o'clock? I usually sleep 'til lunchtime in the summer. Cady does, too, I'll bet."

"Yeah, I don't want to see her today," Sara adds.

Luisa snickers. "Why? She's your new best friend."

"Please!"

"I don't want to see her, either," I tell them. "She'd try to stop us from going across the lake, which we've got to do. You won't believe what's over there. Ready for a shock of major proportions?"

"Lions and tigers and bears?" Sara asks.

"No, nothing like that." I'm trying to keep it light because I know how the graves of so many girls our age will shake them to their bones. "Remember not to pet raccoons or eat belladonna berries on the way."

"Don't worry. I don't eat anything wild or unwashed," Sara says as we trudge on.

She's out of breath before we even reach the cabin, but Luisa forges ahead, and with my short stubby legs I can barely keep up with her.

"How much farther?" Sara complains.

I hand her a bottle of icy water and point to the thick growth banking the lake on the other side. "Just past that, and some grass, and an open field. We're coming up to Cady's cabin. Don't make a sound. She might be in there."

I take a quick peek inside. It's empty — even her picnic basket is gone. The only thing I see is a yellow wax puddle on the floor from the fat candle I saw her burning the last time I was here.

Where does she go when she's not here in the cabin? The cemetery? I do *not* want to find her there.

We trudge on, trying to keep up with Luisa's new athletic stride. She waits for us on the other side of the cabin and says, "You started telling us about the ghost in your attic, but we didn't get the full story."

Somehow walking toward a creepy cemetery doesn't seem like the best time to talk about ghosts. "Later, okay?"

We march through the bushes, the tall grass, and the stubby, grazed grass, until I glimpse the gravestones up ahead and my heart clenches, then starts hammering insanely, too wild to stay in my chest.

Luisa stops short. "What are those things?" she asks.

"You'll see in a minute."

Sara clutches my arm. "I don't think I want to."

Doubling back, Luisa grabs Sara's sleeve. "Don't be so jumpy. We got this far. Now we've got to see what's going on here that has Hannah so spooked. Look at her. She's pasty-white."

In fact, I'm feeling a little sick to my stomach. A few more steps, and we're in the midst of the gravestones.

Luisa catches her breath. "It's a cemetery!"

"I've never been in a cemetery," Sara whispers. "Gives me the shivers, like a ghost is walking across my soul."

We all hush our voices out of respect, as if we're in church. Luisa weaves in and out of the headstones, reading the engravings. Slowly she and Sara get the horrible picture . . . *Here in Effigy Lies* . . . Olivia, Clarinda, Cassandra, Bonnie Ava.

"They're all twelve years old," Sara cries. "Who are they?"

Luisa says, "They can't be related, like if a whole town died of a flu epidemic, because look at the years, 1911, 1950, 2008."

"Anybody know what *effigy* means?" asks Sara.

"I looked it up last night." My voice trembles. "It means it's a substitute, not the real thing."

Luisa's eyes are wide as Ritz crackers. "You mean they're not actually buried here? That the graves are empty, or there are stuffed ragdolls or rotting pumpkins or something weird like that representing Cassandra and Olivia and the others in these graves?"

All I can do is nod.

Sara walks carefully between the gravestones. "Look, three more girls. Here's Emily Dalhart, there's Delia Fogelman. Ooh, this looks like the earliest one."

Here Lies
CADENCE STANHOPE
1887–1899

"Cadence Stanhope," Sara murmurs. "She died way back in 1899. Makes me just want to cry — Cadence was twelve, like the others."

"Cady, short for Cadence?" Luisa brushes wild grass off this oldest of the gravestones.

"Could Cadence Stanhope have been our Cady's grandmother or great-grandmother?" Sara asks.

I shake my head. "Cadence Stanhope was twelve when she died. She couldn't have been anybody's grandmother, no matter how many greats back."

"Yeah, right. Well, Cady might have been named for her ancestor anyway," Sara says. "Maybe an aunt or cousin."

I flash on Cady telling me Vivienne was her mother, as impossible as that seems, but still I have a fierce sense that there's a common thread linking Cady, who won't tell me her last name, and Vivienne, and from them to whoever this girl in the grave is.

I stand beside Cadence Stanhope's headstone. "Notice anything different about this one?"

Sara and Luisa glance from one gravestone to the other.

"I don't get it. What?" asks Sara.

Luisa cries, "I see it. Hers is the only grave that doesn't say *Here in Effigy Lies . . .*"

"Meaning, she is actually buried here," Sara says.

I look from Sara to Luisa to the weathered headstone. "Cadence Stanhope's bones are right under our feet at this very moment."

CHAPTER THIRTY-FOUR

WE SIT IN THE GRASS, EACH OF US IN FRONT OF A different tombstone and deep in our own thoughts. Olivia Bainbridge, 1996 to 2008, supports my back. She'd be about Franny's age now, but I don't remember a Bainbridge family living in Dalton. They could have moved away after Olivia died. When she was ten or eleven, what did she dream for her future? Did she want to be a movie star? A brain surgeon? Did she have brothers and sisters? A pet iguana? What was her room like? Was it full of posters, books, banners, a stuffed giraffe, or a patchwork comforter? Bainbridge sounds like an English name, or maybe Scottish. Were her great-grandparents immigrants?

What did Olivia die of? That's the big question.

Sara breaks the silence. "Think what it must have been like for the parents of Clarinda and Cassandra in 1950, losing two daughters at the same time."

"Bonnie Ava Amberson," Luisa says quietly. "What was going on in the world in 1911 when she died? They were just starting to fly planes. Think she was in a crash of one of those old-fashioned planes with the double set of wings?"

I'm burning with curiosity about these girls, yet my heart feels like it's filled with chilled pebbles. "So many years separate their deaths, and none of them is actually buried here, except for Cadence. Why is that?"

Luisa comes up with an idea. "Wouldn't they be buried where their parents wanted them to rest in peace? Who would want a daughter stuck out here in the middle of nowhere for all eternity?"

"True," Sara agrees, "but then why are their effigies here? And why such a bunch of different years?"

"And why is Cadence Stanhope actually buried in this cemetery?" I ask.

Questions inside of questions, and no answers. "Remember when Mr. Treadwell was talking about World War II and that English prime minister guy, Winston Churchill?"

"Yeah, I remember that video clip he showed us of Churchill's speech, and Mr. Treadwell making a joke about how all newborn babies look like Churchill," Sara says.

"Gracie sure did!"

We all snicker — does it seem disrespectful to laugh while you're leaning on people's gravestones?

Ashamed, I get serious again. "Winston Churchill said something in that speech that's stuck with me like a song you can't get out of your head: *A riddle wrapped in a mystery inside an enigma.* That's what this cemetery is, and everything about Cady, too."

After a while, we get up, brush the grass off our bottoms, and silently find our way back through the grassy field and towering forest. But the riddle wrapped in a mystery inside an enigma is no closer to being solved.

Vivienne, the cameo, Cady, the dead girls, Cadence — Do they all link, like some cosmic paper chain?

�֎ ◎ ✖

"Franny, do you remember having a friend named Olivia when you were in fifth or sixth grade?"

Franny and I are baking brownies to welcome Scooter and Mom and Dad home.

She pops a chunk of walnut into her mouth. "Sort of. It was a long time ago."

"I think her family moved away around 2008. Bainbridge. Olivia Bainbridge."

"I have a spotty memory of someone by that name. I'm getting a bad taste in my mouth, and it's not the brownie dough. Something about Olivia Bainbridge . . ." She shoots cooking spray onto the Pyrex pan. "Here, scrape the batter into the pan and stick it in the oven for twenty-five minutes.

I'm running upstairs to see if I can find my middle school yearbook."

I'm up to my elbows in soap suds and just about have our baking mess cleaned up before Nana Fiona sees it. Warm, sweet smells are coming from the oven as the brownies bake, and then Franny rushes into the kitchen with her yearbook open.

"I remember her now," she says somberly, and she points to a picture of a girl with a pixie haircut and huge, laughing eyes. Below her picture it says,

In Memorium.
April 4, 1996 ~ August 13, 2009

Meaning Olivia Bainbridge is dead. "How did she die?"

Franny shakes her head. "No one really told us. It was summertime, between sixth and seventh grade, so we guessed it was a car crash when her family was on vacation, or maybe she drowned."

Drowned! My heart jerks at that word. "Does her family still live here?"

"I don't think so." Franny pulls out her phone and taps in "Bainbridge Dalton." "Nope, no Bainbridges here now. Sad, isn't it?"

Sadder than she could possibly imagine. My eyes keep drifting back to the yearbook page. Something troubles me about the picture of Olivia. What? *What?* Then it hits me, yes! It says *In Memorium, April 1996 to August 2009.* She had a birthday in 2009, which would make her thirteen when she died, not twelve. But her effigy says 1996 to 2008. How odd is that? Either it's a misprint, or somebody made a big mistake carving her headstone. Which one is wrong?

A half hour later, Mom's SUV comes sputtering into our driveway, and everyone pours into the kitchen, including Trick, who's decided running away to the circus would make it too hard to play third base.

"Scooter!" we all shout. He looks better than he has in months — a few pounds heavier with rosy cheeks. And the best part is, he's not wheezing.

We give hugs all around, though Gracie shyly hangs back. Could she have forgotten Mom and Dad and Scooter in such a short time? Or is she just mad at them for leaving her behind while they went to New Mexico?

Nana grabs Scooter and swings him around the room. "Scott, you are the prince of this castle!"

Trick asks, "When will the brownies be cool enough to snarf?"

And Mom and Dad explain how the hospital in Denver figured out the best way to treat Scooter's asthma. He's to go back every four months for a tune-up.

"We're not moving!" Mom says. "Georgia Dawgs all the way. See, Franny, we'll make it to most of the home games during your freshman year."

"Fab-u-lous," Franny says sarcastically.

"The Studebaker's packed. I'm leaving as soon as the brownies cool. Feels like I'm being sprung from the pokey at long last," Nana Fiona says, but the love in her face, and the *I'll miss you all* in her eyes say the opposite.

Dad kisses her chipmunk cheek, then picks up Gracie, who gives in and nuzzles and slobbers into his ear. "Anything exciting happening around here?" he asks.

"Same old thing," Franny says, slamming her yearbook shut. I notice that she's stuck a napkin as a placeholder on the Olivia Bainbridge page.

Same old thing except a bunch of dead girls and a pinkie promise to go swimming in Moonlight Lake tomorrow night!

CHAPTER THIRTY-FIVE

It sure is easier getting Luisa and Sara up the ladder to the attic this evening than it was getting Nana up here. The family's in the backyard where we can't see them, finishing up a disgusting dinner of fish tacos, which I wouldn't eat if I'd been on a diet of shoe leather all week. The balcony carpenters are done for the day, and their equipment litters the ground like eerie fossils beneath the window. There's an uneasy feeling about the three of us all alone up here.

Once we're nestled on the cushions, with two fans giving some relief in the stifling attic heat, and my blue-shaded lamp generously offering some cozy comfort, I tell them about Vivienne living in this house more than a century ago. "One night, in the middle of a thunderstorm, she was struck blind." I snap my fingers. "Just like that."

"A person doesn't go blind in, well, in the blink of an eye," Luisa protests.

I shrug. "That's the story I heard. You decide what to do with it." Never sure whether Vivienne is listening, I'm careful about my words. I remember how she knocked the cup and saucer out of Nana's hands in fury, though I can't remember what we said to feed her rage.

"Could have been some medical mystery that took her sight," Sara suggests.

I'd been giving this a lot of thought. My brother Trick, who has no curiosity about anything besides food and the life-changing debate over aluminum vs. wooden bats, says I'm a Google junkie, and he's right. So I offer Luisa and Sara my latest theory. "Maybe it wasn't lightning at all, or even night. Say it was no darker than it is right now, but there was an eclipse in the middle of the day. Maybe she looked directly at the sun during totality when it was just a black circle in the sky. That could fry her eyeballs. All I know is what Cady told me . . ."

Ca-dee . . . Ca-dee?

I hear the name drawn out, but neither Luisa's nor Sara's lips move. It must be Vivienne!

Carefully, I continue, "What Cady told me, and what's happened up here in the attic this summer. Even Nana's had a Vivienne experience. Vivienne actually *talked* to Gracie." That should convince them.

Sara's eyes dart around the dark shadows of the attic. "You mean, she's here? The ghost is right here with us?"

Luisa laughs. "You don't believe this stuff, do you? At camp the counselors told scary stories around the campfire, and we all imagined woo-woo spirits rising in the flames, but we knew it was just for fun to spook us before lights-out."

The lamp suddenly sputters. Then when the lightbulb shatters into a zillion slivers of glass, we jump like scared rabbits.

"Whoa!" Sara cries, and Luisa shifts nervously as the attic darkens.

Vivienne's listening, I'm sure of it now. She doesn't know that I've been hanging around with somebody named Cady. And, come to think of it, I never mentioned to Cady that I'd been visited by Vivienne's ghost. Hmm. I sense a few pieces sliding into place like squares on Trick's old Rubik's Cube.

I take the cameo out of my pocket and turn it over so Sara and Luisa can see the initials, V.A.S. "It was hers. Cady told me the V was for Vivienne, but I don't know about the A and the S." And then I get a brilliant idea, another hint toward the missing link of the riddle wrapped in the mystery. "What if the S stands for Stanhope?" As soon as the words are out of my mouth, I'm convinced they're true.

"As in Cadence Stanhope in the cemetery," Sara offers.

"Get real, both of you," Luisa says, rolling her eyes. "Forget the stupid cameo pin. The scary midnight moonlight swim is tomorrow. What are we going to do?"

I'm only half tuned in to the conversation. The other

half of me is scanning every inch of the walls, the rafters, the unloved furniture, searching for Vivienne.

". . . think all those dead girls swam in Moonlight Lake?" Sara asks.

Luisa groans. "Your imagination is in hyperdrive."

I lay the cameo down on the floor beside me. The black onyx profile isn't blinking, the hair ornament is the same as always, and the gold filigree border hasn't changed, though it's not glimmering here in the dusky attic as it would in the brilliant sunlight. But there is something different about it. What is it?

Sara and Luisa chatter on about the midnight swim. Should we or shouldn't we? How would we sneak out of our houses? I'm not listening. Something's nagging at me about the cameo. I can't put my finger on it. And then that's exactly what I do — put my finger on it when I pick it up to look more closely and gasp.

"What?" Sara asks in alarm.

I tap my lips — *shh* — and stare at the cameo and trace it with my fingers to be sure what I see is really there, or actually not there. It's like when you see two cartoons that look just alike, and you have to find the five teensy differences between them. There's only one difference in the cameo: the pearls tight around the woman's throat — they're gone! And then I can't remember for sure that they were ever there.

Vivienne, I say silently, *if you want the cameo back, come and take it. It's yours.*

"Because if those girls are all buried — or, I guess, not buried — in the same place," Sara says, "then maybe all their ghosts are there, and we're . . ."

"There is no such thing as ghosts!" Luisa roars.

At that very moment, a fluttery see-through form floats across the room and fades into nothingness.

Sara whispers, "Did you see . . . ?"

We all gape in disbelief, our three hearts beating to the same terrifying rhythm.

"Vivienne?" I whisper. No answer. "Vivienne!"

And a voice, as thin and fragile as the lightbulb shards on the floor, calls out.

I see all.

Sara clutches her throat, and Luisa slides closer to the fading light from the window.

"See all?" I ask. "But you're blind, aren't you?"

I SEE ALL, the ghost says more emphatically, as if she's annoyed with us for doubting her.

On a hunch, I try out the chant: "*Luisa, Sara, Hannah, and Cady, Midnight moonlight loon nightshady.*"

She repeats it just as I said it!

"I'm not crazy. You both heard it, right?" Sara cries.

"Loon nightshady." I roll that around in my head a while. "Loon-night-shade-y." Then something I hadn't noticed becomes clear. "Our house is called Nightshade, did you know that? But now I also know that it's named after the poisonous belladonna plants that grow in the dark."

"Loon nightshady," Luisa repeats. "What do we know about loons?"

I wake my iPad and click on a YouTube of loon sounds. At low volume, they sound eerie, haunting — like the wails of Nana's banshees foretelling death. At top volume, they explode in our imaginations. In a panic, we scramble to gather our stuff and scuttle down the ladder to the safety of my room.

But a haunting voice trails us just before we slide the ceiling door shut:

Midnight moonlight — NO!

CHAPTER THIRTY-SIX

ALL THREE OF US ARE LYING ON OUR BACKS ACROSS my bed with our legs straight up the wall. Red toenails (Sara), white toenails (Luisa), and blue toenails (me, of course) lined up on the rosy wallpaper.

"We look like a commercial for the Fourth of July," Sara observes, kicking one of Gracie's bean bags across Luisa's feet to mine. It's a game called wall soccer that we invented and we've played since kindergarten. That was before we believed in ghosts.

"Yeah, but it feels more like *Día de los Muertos*," Luisa says. "Day of the Dead. Big in my culture, to remember friends and family who've passed on, wish their souls well on their journey, that sort of thing." She picks up the guitar that Trick and I share. I know about three chords, which is two more than Luisa knows. Plink, pluck, plink, brmmm, and then the same thing over again, as she tunelessly sings a song in Spanish.

"So what are we going to do about the midnight moonlight disaster?" Sara asks. "It's only about twenty-nine hours from now. Twenty-nine hours to our doom, girls!"

"Okay, here's a plan," Sara continues. "I'd never be able to get out of my house at midnight. My parents are practically bloodhounds when it comes to hearing things like a door squeaking open. You'd never get out of your house, either, Luisa, 'cause your parents are total night owls. But here at Hannah's it's always a tornado of activity. Her parents wouldn't notice if we climbed out a third-floor window."

"So why don't we all sleep over here?" Luisa says. "That is, if we're actually going swimming."

I smile. "Even if we don't, it's been forever since we had a sleepover. My dad's got a quadrillion movies we can watch until they go to bed. They usually conk out about eleven o'clock."

Luisa says, "It's a plan!"

Later, after Mom tucks Scooter and Gracie in, she peeks in on us three girls with a hint that it's time for Luisa and Sara to go home before it gets too dark. Then she heads upstairs to work on her "Dear Bettina" column. She's got a letter from a guy engaged to two women named Sandra, and he's having trouble keeping the details of the two weddings straight. What to do? How do people get into messes like that?

But I've got a mess of my own, one that "Dear Bettina" can't solve for me.

Up in the studio the next morning, Dad's got his yellow hardhat on. He's getting ready to go to a new job site. Mr. Mosely's crew finished up with our balcony and has moved on to adding a wing onto a beauty shop called Hairs to You, which sounds like a place where dogs shed a lot, and he's asked Dad to help with the plans. The new sliding door to the balcony is crystal-clear. Glass without Gracie's fingerprints! I slide it open and step onto the balcony with its tiled floor surrounded by a latticed stucco half-wall. Standing here in the cool morning breeze, I try to imagine Vivienne in this space, while she could still see inspiration for her paintings from the brilliant greens and golds of the forest beyond. It's peaceful now. A tiny hummingbird hovers nearby. Vivienne would like this. And then I imagine the horror of losing her sight out here when the black sky ripped open with a burst of jagged light, or was it an eclipse?

I hurry inside, locking the door behind me.

"Hey, Dad, something's on my mind."

"I'm all ears. Hit me."

Ordinarily I'd just reach over and punch his arm as a joke, but today I'm deep in serious thought. "You know your grandparents' old trunk? I got into it and found their wedding picture."

"Handsome couple. Runs in the family," he says, pinching my cheeks.

"How come your grandparents only lived here for a year?"

Dad scratches under the hardhat with a scary architect's tool that looks like something from a torture chamber. "I don't know the whole story, but what I've heard is that they bought the house after the war. That would be World War II, the war *after* the War to End All Wars. The plan was to fill it up with children, like we have. But your Nana Fiona turned out to be their only child, so what did they need with a huge house like this? Talk to Nana about it. Sorry, I gotta get going. Mac Mosely's waiting for me to make a big, expensive decision on that hair place."

Dad's explanation about Cecil and Moira sort of makes sense, but I still wonder. Was there some other reason why they moved in and out so quickly? Could it have been because Vivienne made it impossible for them to stay?

The cool of the morning is my perfect opportunity to dash off to the forest for a few minutes. I've been wondering about Cady's boat, and where she got the planks for it.

It's not hard to figure out as soon as the cabin is in sight. It's leaning toward some trees as if a truck accidentally nudged it off its foundation. Closer up, I see that the whole back side is gone.

"What did you do?" I bellow. There's no answer, not that I expected one. "Cady! Cady!" I call at the top of my lungs, furious that she's destroying this cabin board by board. But then, why should I care? It was just a pile of rotten wood. Still, it was the one thing I could count on being *there*, when Cady wasn't.

I'm answered with silence. When Cady's gone, she is *so* gone, and I have no idea where. What's that weird thing Dad says? *If a tree falls in the forest and no one's there, does it make a sound?*

Moonlight Lake lies a few yards from the cabin. Two ducks lazily swim circles around each other. The lake is calm and beautiful in the thin, early light of day. What will it look like at midnight tonight?

No one's inside what's left of the cabin. If I poked at any of the three remaining walls, the whole thing would crumble. Cady's picnic basket is back on the rickety table, taunting me to open it. Why am I not surprised to see the peach music box Nana Fiona gave me? Glued on the bottom is a metal sticker with my name: Hannah Ruth Flynn. I twist the key, and "Sweet Georgia Brown" fills the empty room as the peach slowly revolves.

Cady's been here this morning, which I can tell by the fact that another fat yellow candle is burning on top of the dried wax in the center of the floor. Should I blow it out? The candle flame is flickering, fluttering toward the open space.

An ominous feeling prickles my skin, and I tear out of the cabin so fast that my feet can barely catch up with the rest of my body. I shoot like an arrow straight out of the forest. I hate this place. I'll never come back!

A sharp, choking smell hits me when I'm safely to the fallen log at the edge of the woods. Shading my eyes, I peer back between pines and live oaks and cottonwoods thick with mid-summer growth. Smoke is pluming in dark clouds, and I know deep in my soul that the cabin is burning to the ground. My music box! I pray that the fire doesn't jump toward the trees or toward the gentle animals that own the forest. *They* own it, not Cady.

CHAPTER THIRTY-SEVEN

AN HOUR LATER I CAN STILL CATCH WHIFFS OF THE smoke. It stings my nose and makes me furious. But I've got to focus on solving the mystery instead of that burnt up old cabin that never meant anything to me anyway.

"Hey, Trick, can I borrow one of your Rubik's Cubes?"

"Get your own," he mutters, even as he tosses me his favorite one. That's Trick for you, gruff on the outside and mushy inside. In fact, he's the opposite of Scooter, who's gentle and tender outside, but his interior is steely and stronger than anybody I know.

I take the cube back to my room, kicking the door shut. Scooter's waiting for me to fill him in on things he's missed while he was away. I clue him in on everything I know about Cady so far, though he hasn't seen the actual graveyard and doesn't want to. He fiddles with the Rubik's Cube, trying to line up the colors like the champs you see on YouTube who can solve the puzzle in five seconds. He's good, but not that good.

"Sure glad the whole forest didn't go up in flames," Scooter says reassuringly.

"Just the cabin. Miraculous, isn't it, that the fire burned out so quickly? But then, Cady does a lot of things we can't explain. Pass me the Rubik's Cube, Scooter." Randomly, I slide colors around, getting no closer to lining up all the yellows, reds, blues, greens, oranges, and whites on their own sides of the cube. But just slowly pivoting a multicolored panel of tiles helps me concentrate on clicking into place pieces of the riddle wrapped in a mystery.

Scooter grabs the cube away from me again and starts twisting. "Facts: what do we know about Cady? Let's call her Orange on this cube. We'll try to solve her. It fits because orange doesn't rhyme with anything, just like she doesn't fit into normal life any which way you try to wedge her in." He flashes an all-orange side of the cube.

"Okay, facts. She can't keep her stories straight," I tell him.

"Say it right out. She lies."

"I don't want to say it. Fact: she has six empty graves in her cemetery, and one that's got a customer in it, and that would be some relative from way back named Cadence Stanhope."

"That she's probably named after," Scooter reminds me.

"Fact: she wants Sara and Luisa and me to come swimming at midnight tonight. What'll we do about that?"

Scooter makes eyeglasses out of his index fingers and thumbs and gazes at me through them. "If I could see into ze future," he says, in a fake fortune-teller accent, "I vould say do not go to ze lake at ze midnight."

"Like Vivienne said — NO!"

"We haven't gotten to Vivienne yet. Stick with Orange."

"So Orange knows an awful lot about the forest and doesn't get sick on poisonous berries or raccoon scratches like regular people do. She appears and disappears whenever she feels like it."

Scooter slides the cube fast a bunch of times and gets the colors all mixed up again. "She knows way more than she should about Nightshade, the house, and the poison. Gives me the creeps."

"And a lot about Vivienne and how she stood on the balcony of her studio, Dad's studio, and suddenly her lights went out."

"Blind as a bat."

That triggers something in my mind. "Cady went ballistic when she saw the carpenters repairing the balcony. That's got to be a key to . . . something."

"Let's move on to Vivienne," Scooter says. "She's Red. All we really know about her is what Cady told you, which may or may not be true."

"Except that she's haunting our house."

"Like I said, which may or may not be true."

"It's true, believe me. Nana knows it. Even Gracie saw her. Sara and Luisa sort of did, too."

We're silent, barely moving for a few minutes while Scooter twists and solves, and finishes the cube again, but we're no closer to solving our puzzle.

Suddenly his back shoots up straight and he tosses the cube in the air. "Think it's a coincidence that Cady warned you not to fix the balcony, and that Vivienne warned you not to go for the midnight moonlight swim?"

"Coincidence? Hmm, maybe not, but why does *that* matter?"

Scooter says, "They hate each other?"

"Or love each other and just hate me."

"I don't think so. Maybe this sounds like a comic book, but what if Vivienne knows Cady's power, and Cady knows Vivienne's power, and each one is trying to protect you from the other one?"

"Wow, maybe you're on to something, Scooter. That means we'd sure better not do the midnight moonlight thing. It's settled. I'll text Sara and Luisa in a minute."

He tilts the cube back and forth so the overhead light picks up the glossy red side, then the glossy orange . . . red . . . orange.

"So next question," I begin, "Yellow: how are Cady and

Vivienne related? Remember, Cady tried to convince me that Vivienne was her mother with that crazy stuff about time being twisted and rippled like a ball of yarn."

"Yeah, but time *isn't* rippled," Scooter asserts. "It's a straight line from point A to point B, from noon to one second past noon."

I'm brewing a thought that I can only grasp around the edges before it poofs away in a mind mist. "Stick with me on this Scooter, because I'm not sure what I'm saying. So if Vivienne is the ghost of someone who died in 1899, and time is all tangled up, why can't Cady —"

"Be a ghost, too, just like Vivienne," Scooter says.

"Maybe she really *was* the daughter of Vivienne."

We look at each other, our eyes gaping wide at this absolutely insane idea and both say, at the exact same time, "Naaah, no way."

"You got a better theory?" Scooter asks, and I have to admit I don't, but I know for sure this one can't possibly be right.

CHAPTER THIRTY-EIGHT

IT'S FINALLY SATURDAY NIGHT. TRICK'S UP IN HIS room with the door locked, Scooter's asleep (though he's prepared to cover for me, if necessary), and Gracie's been in dreamland since eight o'clock. But wouldn't you know it? This is the first Saturday night Franny's had off from the Rib Shack all summer. When Sara and Luisa arrive, sleeping bags and munchies and all, Franny says, "I'll hang out with you. Slum a little for a change."

Great. So how are we going to discuss Cady? It's almost ten o'clock. Two hours to midnight. We're wrecks, skittish and jittery. Sara's chewing on the fringe of a couch cushion, and Luisa's fidgeting with her toes as if she's lost count of how many there are.

We're in our pajamas, camped out in the family room with a movie on the wide-screen TV. There's a big, beach-ball full moon out there, as Cady promised, and I feel it pulling me like it pulls the tides. Cady's out there all by herself, waiting for us. She's as lonely as the moon so far away from all those twinkly stars.

"Gorgeous moon," Franny says. "It's so romantic, or it would be if Cameron hadn't dumped me last week. I don't care. I was ready to move on anyway. Off to college in forty-two days."

Our eyes are glued to the screen. We're ignoring her, so maybe she'll take the hint and go upstairs.

But no. "You know what they say about a big full moon? It drives people crazy."

Sara darts a nervous look my way as Franny says, "I'm going into the kitchen to make Rice Krispies Treats. Anyone want to help?"

"Huh-uh." Luisa and Sara and I all exchange looks: our chance! Even though we'd already decided not to go tonight, we're all prepared . . . just in case we change our minds. As soon as Franny is out of earshot, we huddle.

"Got your suits and towels?"

"Out on the porch for a quick getaway."

"If we're going."

"Which we're not."

"Cady needs us to come."

"Which we won't."

"But if we do . . ."

"Flashlights? Bug spray? Mosquitoes are vicious at night around water."

"We shouldn't go."

"But we can't disappoint Cady."

"This is crazy!"

"We wouldn't consider it if we had an ounce, even a milliliter of good sense."

"Which we don't."

"But if we did . . ."

Franny pops back into the family room, rattling a cereal box. "It's practically empty," she says with disgust. "You can't make Rice Krispies Treats without Rice Krispies."

Luisa chirps, "Why don't you go to the store for another box? And can you get us a giant bag of turkey jerky?"

"Yeah, great idea!" we chorus.

"Nah, I don't need the calories," Franny responds, curling into the corner of the couch with her laptop open.

"Can't you do that somewhere else?" I whine. "Your computer light's bothering us. What do you think, Luisa, you're right next to her. Bothering you?"

"Majorly," Luisa shouts, covering her eyes with a pillow as if Franny's pointing a 2000-watt searchlight at her.

"Just checking one thing quick. There, I'm done," and Franny flips the laptop shut.

The clock's ticking. It's nearly ten-thirty, and we haven't reached a decision. Cady must be feeling desperate, wondering if we'll come or not. Mom and Dad are still awake upstairs. My nerves are a jangled army marching across the bottom of my stomach.

And then, we're saved. Franny yawns. "Sleepovers used to be a lot more fun when I was a kid. I'm outta here. *Hasta la vista,* girls!" She tosses the purple and green afghan, one of Nana's uglier ones, on the floor and heads upstairs.

Then the huddle begins for real.

"Think about how sad Cady is. We're the only friends she has," I begin.

"She hasn't got me," Sara says.

Luisa shakes her head. "Me, neither."

"Have a heart," I say.

Sara looks me dead in the eye. "Look at it from a practical point of view. What if we stumble in the dark and break a leg? How are we gonna explain it to our parents in the emergency room?"

"Or what if we accidentally swallow some belladonna and croak right there in the woods, and nobody finds us for, like, twenty-five years," Luisa moans.

"What if we get bitten by a possum or a raccoon or bear? Are there bears in the forest? Do they hibernate at night?" Sara is on a roll. "Black widow spiders, brown recluse spiders, they can totally kill, and you wouldn't see them in the dark before they took a chunk of your flesh."

Then Luisa points out what's really on our minds. "What if we drown? What if there are three more graves dug next to Olivia and Cassandra and those other girls?"

"Ours," I whisper.

We sit in stunned silence, contemplating this and all the other what-ifs, until Sara says, "Look, it's okay if y'all don't speak to me for the rest of the summer and all through seventh grade, but I'm not going."

Luisa quickly chimes in. "This is kind of terrifying. I mean, think about it. Three girls out at midnight, hanging around with that total headcase, Cady. And, to be honest, I'm not a great swimmer. They made me wear a float donut at camp."

"So you're not going, either?" asks Sara.

"That's two out of three," Luisa says, casting me an expectant look.

They wait while I try to make up my mind. One minute, I'm going to the lake. The next, I'm not. I know I need to give them my decision. If I can figure out what it is.

CHAPTER THIRTY-NINE

I HIT PAUSE ON THE MOVIE. WE'RE ALL YAWNING. I blow an imaginary bugle, then poke the air with a double thumbs-down. "Announcement, cadets, this just in from Mission Control. The mission is scrapped. It's a no-go."

Luisa and Sara both let out a huge sigh of relief, like my own.

"I'll be asleep in two secs," Luisa promises. Her long legs are coiled in Dad's overstuffed chair, her head thrown back, her mouth open wide enough to catch dragonflies. Sara snuggles down into her sleeping bag with a pillow over her head, and in a flash her back is rising up and down in peaceful sleep, like hibernation. How can they both be out so fast, with a clear conscience?

I'm the night owl, wide-awake. I click off the TV and plop down on the couch, shielding my eyes from the yellow beam of Luisa's flashlight and counting the ticks of the wall clock. It's eleven thirty-eight. I picture Cady's expectant face. She's waiting for us on the shore, backlit by the powerful moon. What's that word she used to describe the moon? Oh, yeah, *lambent.* I looked it up and found out it has nothing to do with sheep. It means glowing. The glowing, radiant moon. Luna. Waiting for Luisa and Sara and me. Well, Luna's going to have a long wait!

My eyes are wide open; they're on springs. I'm staring at the ceiling, counting spins of the fan whooshing overhead. I force my heavy eyelids closed. The ceiling and the clock are visible through narrow slits. From a great distance, as though it's funneled down a skinny tube of time and space, I imagine Cady's voice:

Let those cowards sleep. You're the one with courage, Hannah.

In the back of my mind, I hear my father's constant message to all five of us: "When in doubt, do the *right thing,* even if what's right feels wrong." I never quite knew what he meant until this minute, and now I'm having second thoughts about my decision.

It cracks my heart in two to think of disappointing poor Cady. I know how I'd feel if I were the one out there, all by myself in the moonlight. I can't do it. I can't abandon Cady this way.

I'm going alone.

Like that, I'm on my feet and out the door. I grab one of the flashlights stashed on the porch and head out into the night. I'm following someone's footsteps — my own? — one foot after the next. Going where? Eyes wide open. Spectral night vision. Thin loblolly pines jut a hundred feet into the air. Thick cottonwoods surround me. They're havens for small creatures. Eyes watch me pass; they know exactly where I'm going.

A thin wail in the distance cuts through the natter of forest night noise. Is it a trapped cat? A loon? The full moon floods my path. Crushed pine needles crunch under my feet. Why didn't I think to wear shoes? I walk and walk, afraid I'll never get there, and then I hear her:

"Hannah! You came. You really are an honest and true friend."

"I can't see you, Cady."

"Because I'm wearing black, and the moon has slipped behind a cloud. Keep following my voice." It's a soothing, inviting voice, a mother's lullaby. "Come, Hannah. I'm here at the lake. Let's swim together by moonlight. Hurry. It's nearly midnight."

The voice is a rope that gently tugs me forward. No, it's too soft to be a rope. It's a long, white silk string — like the one that linked Moira's wedding pearls. It's tied around my heart like a kite string. I'm flying, with my feet on the ground.

"Just a few more steps into the water, Hannah. Dip your toes in. Ahh. It's refreshing, right? Feel the soft silt squishy under your feet? Such a lovely feeling. A few more steps. Wade toward me. That's it, yes, this way."

Midnight water cools my stinging feet. My legs. My knees. My thighs. Something swims and floats around me: my pajama T-shirt. The water's up to my waist, and now the shirt clings to my sides. I'm practically swimming. I can't call it wading anymore, not this deep. But I'm getting no closer to the unseen voice.

"Over here." Cady calls to me from farther and farther away. "My friends are waiting to meet you."

"I'm coming, Cady. Stand still so I can find you."

"Just trust me," she calls across the water, which jingles a little alarm in my head. My father always says something else that seems relevant, but I can't think what it is because each step is a huge struggle. I'm dragging dead weight, like trudging through a bank of snow.

Soft ground slides away under my feet. The water lies heavy on my chest, then my throat. Wet hair slaps my neck. How can something as silky as water weigh so much?

The loon's wail contradicts Cady's soothing voice. "I'm here, I won't let anything hurt you, Hannah. We come from water, and return to water."

The loon is nearly screeching now. Have I upset its nest of babies? Its wail means something important, but what? I know the answer, but I can't pull that out of my memory, either. Everything's dreamy and hazy, and breathing takes every ounce of my strength.

My whole body shudders with a deep, cleansing breath. And now the water feels so welcoming, so comforting, so natural. Peaceful. Mosquitoes circle my face and nip at my cheeks. It doesn't matter. *We come from water, and return to water.*

Must be midnight by now. *Midnight moonlight loon night-shady.* I'm blinded by the glaring light of the full moon. Blinded . . . like Vivienne.

But only for a moment. I blink to clear my eyes — and my mind. I suddenly *know* that it's not a loon I hear. It's a banshee wail, warning that someone is struggling into the world beyond just as I'm slogging through this cold water. Who would that be? I'm the only one here besides Cady. "Where *are* you?" I call. But I get no answer from her.

I'm starting to panic, and butterflying my legs to propel my body out of the water, but my legs are anchors, my arms are lead. They don't work.

Finally, Cady wades toward me. But how can she stand, when the water's nearly over my head and she's no taller than I am? Suddenly she grabs my hands and pulls ferociously. I'm too weak to resist. My head goes under. My breathing is ragged, like how Scooter feels during an asthma attack. I'm choking! I force my exhausted legs to pump and thrust my head out of the water, spitting and drawing gulps of air. But Cady's gone under the water, and she's towing me down.

Why is she doing this?

CHAPTER FORTY

IN MY HEAD, VIVIENNE'S VOICE SCREAMS, *NO!*

No *what?*

Cady keeps tugging at me beneath the weight of the lake. I know *what* now! With inhuman strength, I pump and thrash and kick until my head is out of the water again. It's a tug-of-war between Cady and me. Again and again I break loose, my hair whipping around my face. I'm so tired. My whole body goes limp with exhaustion.

Someone else is in the water! I don't want it to be one of Cady's friends. I can't battle two of them. So why resist any longer? It'd be easy to just give myself over to the water and moonlight.

Behind me, wild splashes come closer, and a voice that's not Cady's floats across Moonlight Lake. "Hold on, Hannah, we're coming." It's Sara!

"I'm doing the best I can," Luisa says, gasping and sucking air, "but like I said, I'm not a great swimmer."

With my last burst of energy, I pivot my body around to see Sara and Luisa wrestle the lake, with their arms slashing through the water, their feet kicking like mermaid fins.

Cady's head darts out of the water between Sara and me without causing so much as a ripple in the lake.

An arm slips around my waist. Luisa's, not Cady's! Sara is on the other side of me, bearing most of the weight, free-styling with her other arm and kicking like mad. A cloud slides away, and in the harsh moonlight Cady's eyes are fierce and feverish. She's neck-deep in the water and motionless, even though she can't be standing on anything.

Luisa and Sara swim me to the shore, and all three of us collapse in the soft mud, panting and coughing. My heart's slowing down a little, and my eyes begin to shed the sting-ing lake water, until Cady's face, contorted in fury, looms over our shivering bodies.

In a rage, she's sputtering frenzied words: "I invited you all to come, but y'all are cowards. Only Hannah is worthy. You spoiled everything."

Cady is wearing sweatpants and a black hoodie, not a swimsuit. Somehow her clothes and hair are perfectly dry. And then she's gone. Poof.

"Where did she go?" Sara asks. She's the fastest of us to recover. Luisa's totally wiped out, and I'm not exactly danc-ing on the shore myself.

The banshee wail — or was it the loon's call — is silent now, as if the whole forest is holding its breath. I sit up and look around. Cady's nowhere in sight. "She comes and goes like *that*," I say, snapping my fingers. "Where would I be if y'all hadn't swum out to rescue me?"

Sara and Luisa exchange looks, but neither says what we're all thinking: *I'd be headed for one of those graves.* I'm sure, now. Cady meant to drown me in Moonlight Lake.

"How did you know to come?" I ask Sara and Luisa.

"Scooter. The little twerp set his alarm for eleven forty-five, because he was curious to see whether we'd be going at midnight." Luisa sinks back, still exhausted.

Sara fills in the details. "When he saw that you'd gone alone, he panicked and shook us awake. He gave us a head start before he woke your parents. I hope they didn't call mine yet! All the parents will be basket cases by the time they see our faces." Sara stretches out one hand to Luisa and the other to me, pulling us up, and we head for home with mud glued to our backs and water dribbling down our legs.

"Who is Cady, really?" Luisa asks, but we all suspect the answer. The girl who can appear and vanish in a flash; who can stand in water above her head; who can swim in the moonlight and come up desert-dry. The girl who survives poison berries; who talks about tangled time; whose friends are all dead and buried . . .

"She's some kind of a witch," Sara says as we come close to the fallen log at the mouth of the forest.

Luisa's idea is more shocking: "She's Cadence Stanhope, and she's buried out there in her little cemetery."

Then I say what we're all thinking. "She's a ghost."

CHAPTER FORTY-ONE

MOM AND DAD AND SCOOTER MEET US HALFWAY back to Nightshade, with towels and blankets and hugs and tears. They'll yell at us later for doing such a stupid thing, I'm sure, but right now they're just grateful that we're on our feet and breathing.

We dump our wet, muddy clothes in the washing machine and change into dry things, and then Mom's interrogation begins.

"What were y'all *thinking*!"

It's not easy to explain, but we try, and they listen. I tell them the easy stuff that won't make them totally crazy right away, about meeting Cady, and how lonely she was — and so was I with my best friends gone and Scooter getting sicker and Franny ready to leave for college. I tell them about the cabin that burned and the cameo, the poisoned belladonna berries, and how Nightshade got its name.

Dad's face is full of questions. "You're saying that your new friend Cady lives in the forest? That she's been enticing you to play with her, and you've done it, even though it's against the rules?"

Play with her sounds so babyish, but it's a pretty accurate description. Miserably, I nod. "Yes, but . . ."

"I'm not through, Hannah. So all she had to do was invite you to come swimming at midnight. Midnight, Hannah! And you did it! Do you realize how foolish, how dangerous that is? You could have drowned."

My heart beats frantically in my ears, because he's so close to the truth.

Luisa and Sara have the good sense to keep quiet while they wait for their parents to arrive with zillions of questions of their own.

I take a deep breath, and glance over at Scooter. His eyebrows are raised with questions, too.

A stuttering tape plays and rewinds and plays again in my mind: *Luisa, Sara, Hannah, and Cady . . . Midnight moonlight loon nightshady.* "I know it sounds insane," I tell my parents, "but Cady was unbelievably persuasive about the midnight swim. None of us really wanted to do it."

"Yet you did," Dad says again. His tone surprises me, because he hardly ever gets mad. It's because he's so worried about me.

"I couldn't bear to disappoint Cady. She really, really needed a friend. So did I," I murmur, avoiding Sara's and

Luisa's eyes. "I just couldn't let her down. Remember what you always tell us about doing the right thing, Dad? Even if it seems wrong? After Luisa and Sara fell asleep, I did what I thought was right. Cady and I, we were . . . friends. I imagined her voice calling me, and so did the loons."

"The loons?" Mom asks, as though this is the craziest thing I've said all night.

"Yes, the wail of the loons kept drawing me closer and closer to the water, and then Cady's voice drew me deep into Moonlight Lake until I was in over my head."

Mom gasps and tucks her lips into her teeth to keep from saying what's on the tip of her tongue. Whatever it is, she knows I don't want to hear it right now.

Sara can't hold her tongue any longer. "Cady isn't like a normal kid, Mr. and Mrs. Flynn."

"No, I guess not," Dad says sadly.

Scooter catches my eye and jerks his head toward our parents, as if to say, *Go ahead, tell them the rest.*

A gob of spit hangs in my throat, which I swallow and say, "There's a small cemetery on the other side of the lake." Sara and Luisa look shocked that I'd mention this. But I can't stop now. "There are seven graves there." My throat tightens. This will scare Mom and Dad out of their skins. "All of the graves are for girls my age."

Mom clutches her throat. "Seven dead children? Good Lord!"

"Yes, but six are effigies," Luisa says, and my parents' eyes turn toward her.

"Which means that those girls aren't actually buried there," I quickly explain, as if this is really going to comfort Mom and Dad.

"And the seventh?" Mom asks.

I glance at Luisa and Sara again, and they both close their eyes. "The seventh is Cadence Stanhope, who *is* buried there."

Scooter's been chomping to jump into the conversation. This is his chance. "Y'all get it? Cadence . . . Cady?"

Mom's eyes widen with confusion, and Dad's pressing me for more.

"Let me see if I understand this. You're telling us that your friend Cady who lives in the forest is . . . dead? That a ghost has been talking to you all summer? That's a little hard to swallow," he says, sinking back into his easy chair.

"I know, Dad, but look at the facts. Isn't that something else you're always telling us?"

He lurches forward. "The *fact* is that this Cady is a mentally disturbed child. The *fact* is that you let her lure you into the forest again and again, when you should have known better and should have told us what was going on. Couldn't you trust us to help? This child needs help, Hannah."

"She's dead, Mom and Dad. Dead! Get it? She's a ghost!"

All six of us sit in silence, with the words *dead* and *ghost* ping-ponging off the walls until Sara and Luisa's parents arrive and we have to go through the whole thing again.

CHAPTER FORTY-TWO

LUISA AND SARA AND THEIR PARENTS ARE GONE.
Scooter's been sent up to his room. It's just Mom and Dad
and me in the living room.

"I'm really tired. Can I go to bed?"

Mom says, "Yes, we're all exhausted. We'll talk more
tomorrow."

I'll bet we will! I bolt out of the room fast enough to
beat my shadow to the stairs.

Scooter is crouching behind a chair on the second floor
landing.

"You heard the whole thing?"

"Missed a word or two," Scooter admits. "I've gotta talk
to you."

Upstairs in my room, we huddle on the floor, leaning
against my bed, and Scooter dumbfounds me with his
news.

"While you were at that happy little swim party, I was
taking care of business in the attic."

"Scooter, no! There's so much dust up there!"

"It's okay. The new meds are helping a lot. I told myself, if I think hard enough, Vivienne will talk to me, and she did."

My jaw drops. "Just like *that*?"

"Not the way you think. Hey, you should have swept up the glass from the broken lightbulb and tea cup. I could have made hamburger out of my bare feet. Anyway, I found your iPad up there. Why didn't we think of Googling stuff about Vivienne, if she was this hotshot artist?"

"Find out anything interesting?"

"Plenty. You really want to know?" Scooter teases. "Maybe I'll just go to bed and tell you in the morning."

"It's *already* morning. Talk!"

He shifts around, pulls a foam pillow off my bed, and stretches out on the floor. His words float up toward the ceiling, but I snatch them out of the air.

"They both died the same night, Vivienne and Cady."

"How horrible for poor Anthony, losing his wife and daughter on the same night."

"Ah, *bzzzzz*, wrong answer. He was Vivienne's husband, but not Cady's father."

"He wasn't?" I ask.

"And Vivienne wasn't Cady's mother."

"What? She lied about that, too? How do you know all this?"

"I'm trying to tell you. It was 1898, three years after Autumn Splendor, also known as Nightshade, was built, and a year before Vivienne went blind. And incidentally, she swears it was because of that bolt of lightning, which doesn't seem possible, since the lightning never touched her."

"Yeah, that's what Cady said, but we've already established that she plays loose with the truth."

"Here's the weird part. Vivienne let me know that she was there with me. The lamp flickered on."

"Without a lightbulb!"

"Right-o. Clear sign, wouldn't you say? Not that I saw anything like a real body. But she was moving around so quickly that my hair was blowing in the draft she caused. Her thoughts were pinging me from this corner, that corner, from under the chair with the stuffing hanging out, from the shelf by the window. The mice got your Cheetos, by the way."

"Who cares about the Cheetos. What was she saying?"

"Nothing . . . until I told her that you were swimming at midnight with Cady, and she screamed 'NO!'"

"I heard her say that once, too!"

"Then your iPad started blinking like a railroad stop light, and blue links flashed across the screen, dozens of them. And then everything went blank, except one website lit up in a highlight color I've never seen before, a bright sparkly silvery-blue like water."

"You clicked on it?" I ask, breathlessly.

"That's how I got the whole scoop. Cady was her

husband's niece who came to live with the family just before Vivienne went blind. And Cady didn't fit in with the family. There were three other kids, two older and one younger. Cady did nasty stuff, like hiding a dead rat under the little kid's pillow, and throwing soup at the walls in the dining room. She stole their stuff and hid it in the forest."

"Like my nail polish and my Sweet Georgia Brown music box!"

"It gets worse. She tried to feed the other kids those belladonna berries, but they never trusted anything she said or did, which is why they didn't drop dead. Cady and Vivienne were like cats and dogs, hissing and barking at each other even before Vivienne went blind. Afterward it was worse."

"Yeah, Cady told me even the dog was a wreck."

"There was no dog. Cady wanted a dog, but Vivienne said no way, because there were already too many things for her to trip over. Cady was always leaving things in Vivienne's path. She was a real pain, wasn't she?"

"Still is," I say softly, but I wonder if *is* implies living, whereas Cady *isn't*.

Scooter continues in rapid-fire bursts of information. "One night, way back then, Vivienne was standing on the balcony, the one outside Dad's studio. She couldn't see her hand in front of her eyes, or anything else, but she hung around out there imagining the twinkling stars and planets.

Cady came out to the balcony, but she wouldn't say who she was. Another one of her mean tricks. To Vivienne, it was pitch-black on the small balcony, and she didn't know who she was bumping shoulders with. So she reached out to flap her hand around Cady's face, to figure out who it was. Cady wasn't gonna let Vivienne paw her, so she leaned away and backed against the little low wall, and then it kinda went downhill from there."

"You mean they had a real knock-down, drag-out fight?" I ask.

"No, when Cady jerked away from Vivienne, the whole balcony went *downhill* because it was built by carpenters with sawdust and spackle for brains."

"Do we know what happened next?"

"Vivienne lost her balance and both of them tumbled over the wall."

"Or the floor collapsed under them," I suggest. "Whatever happened, they both crashed into the pool below the balcony. Did you know there used to be a pool in our yard?"

"Yeah, but not the kind of pool where you can just swim away like a stunned eel. The water was shallow. There would've been just enough to drown in. Or maybe their heads bashed into the concrete before they had a chance to drown. The fact is, they both died, and Vivienne blames herself. Oh, and one other thing," Scooter says with a sheepish grin. "Your iPad is totally blown. It's deader than a popped balloon."

CHAPTER FORTY-THREE

MY MIND RACES THROUGH THE MENU SWARMING in my head. "Why did Vivienne shatter the lightbulb and Nana Fiona's tea cup?"

Scooter twists his mouth in thought. "Theory Number One: maybe she just wanted us to know she's there. Not even a cockroach likes being ignored."

"Yeah, but there's got to be some other reason, something more . . . ghostly."

An apple on my desk tempts Scooter. His biting and crunching drive me crazy, because I want to hear more. Instead, what I get is, "If I swallow the seeds, think an orchard will grow in my gut?"

"Forget the apples. What do you think about Vivienne?"

"Theory Number Two: she wants our help."

"What for?"

"I don't know. To settle some mess?" Scooter spits the seeds halfway across the room toward my trash can and misses. In a hundred years this spot will be an orchard. "Here's the way I figure it," Scooter says. "Cady blames

Vivienne and Vivienne blames herself for the balcony thing, or maybe it's the other way around."

"That means one's hissing-mad, and the other's burning up with guilt," I speculate.

"Get over it. More than a century's passed already."

"Their souls are locked in eternal battle. How sad is that, Scooter?"

"Theory Number Three: after they bump into each other in the world beyond, they strike a deal — Vivienne gets Nightshade. Cady lives in the forest and stays away from our house."

"She got in here at least twice — once to steal my things and once to move that cameo around."

He shrugs. "Okay, she swings by every so often for kicks, but she doesn't hang out here, right?"

"Because she doesn't want to run into Vivienne, and Vivienne never sets foot in Cady's forest."

Scooter gets a faraway look in his eye. "If we don't do something to fix things between them, they could go on hating each other forever."

❧ ◉ ❧

Last night, Mom said that we'd talk some more about my adventure — near-death experience, she calls it — and today we've talked about it until I'm so bored I could spit. I'm never to go back to the forest under any circumstances, not to talk to Cady, not to swim at all until further notice, not even in the kiddie pool at the country club, and not to go out after dark without one or more chaperones over the age of eighteen. Meaning Mom and Dad, who would be happy if I stayed in my room under house arrest with one of those ankle cuffs for the next thirty years.

Luisa and Sara are under the same reign of terror at their houses. We have been called irresponsible. Foolhardy. Defiant. Untrustworthy. Lucky to be alive. I feel badly that I've gotten them into this mess. And I can't stop thinking about those moments in Midnight Lake: clenching my teeth until my jaws ache so I can't swallow water, feeling it crawl into my lungs through my nose anyway; gasping for breath whenever I come up for air, sinking back under the surface no matter how hard I try not to; feeling my leaden legs and arms refuse to pump. And all the while hearing the wail of the banshee loon growing more frantic until it's nearly screeching its warning.

So, yeah, I'm lucky to be alive. But that doesn't mean I'm through with Cady. I have too many unanswered questions, especially now that I know Vivienne's story. I'm pretty sure hers and Cady's won't be tight-fitting jigsaw pieces. I have to find out. Today.

I peek into Dad's studio. He's so engrossed at his drafting table that he doesn't hear or see me. With a start, I notice that the door to the new balcony is open, and I think of its wall and floor giving way in 1899, plunging Vivienne and Cady into the pool below.

Mom's down in the kitchen concocting one of her disgusting green energy drinks, and the blender is roaring. Perfect. The bathroom window slides open smoothly, as if it's telling me it's okay. If it didn't want me to sneak out of the house, it would have stuck like it usually does. I hang my legs outside. It's only the second floor, but it seems like a long way down to the ground when you have to jump.

I slither down a drainpipe toward the first floor. Wish I'd thought to put on jeans instead of shorts because I'm scraping half my leg skin off. There goes my summer tan. I'm holding on by white knuckles. A few more inches . . . a few more and I can leap to the ground. For somebody who's supposed to be smart, I forgot that there's no cushy grass below this window. Nope, it's a hedge of prickly blackberry. Ouch. Ouch!

Gingerly, I tear my way through the bush and run toward the forest, pulling spiky blackberry thorns out of my legs and tossing them to the wind. The blackberry I've popped into my mouth is about three days short of being ripe, and I spit the mash to the ground just as I reach the fallen log at the entrance to the forest. Today no barrier can stop me. I'm an Olympic sprinter jumping over a hurdle, running toward the lake. I grind to a halt where the cabin once stood. The ash is still smoldering like coals in a barbecue pit.

At the top of my lungs, I holler her name: "CADENCE STANHOPE!" There's nothing here among the trees to echo my bellow. "Cady! Cadence Stanhope, I know all about you. Vivienne told me everything, every single thing." Okay, it's not quite the truth, but she'll want to defend herself, and besides, I'm desperate as I dash around the lake and barrel toward the cemetery.

When I get close to it, my throat tightens. I don't want to see those gravestones. I don't want to think about those girls, Olivia and Clarinda and Cassandra and the others who all — yes, I'm sure of it now — who all drowned. As I was supposed to do.

Here I am, suddenly in the midst of the graves. The blazing noonday sun torments me, searing my face and urging me to run back into the sheltering shade of the cottonwoods and pines. Forget the graves, it tells me. Forget Cady. Sweat pools down my back. I squint in the unforgiving sunlight, wishing I'd been smart enough to wear sunglasses, or a baseball cap with a visor. Wishing I were anywhere but here.

But *here* is where I need to be. I drop to the grass, my back ramrod straight against the gravestone that reads, *Here lies Cadence Stanhope.* I expect the granite to be hot, sizzling in the sun all these hours, but it's not, and I put my fiery cheek against the cold stone for comfort.

Comfort? In a graveyard? Talk about creepy.

CHAPTER FORTY-FOUR

How long does it take for a body to disintegrate in the earth? Cady's been in that grave for about a hundred and twenty years. There must be nothing left but a skeleton, a skull with teeth bigger than you ever expect, and maybe a few wisps of cloth, which outlasts flesh. If that's all that's left of Cady, how does she materialize into something solid, someone who looks so . . . alive?

"I *am* alive." The voice comes from behind me and Cady steps around to the front of her gravestone. "I'm alive because you need to see me this way. Do you know how much energy it takes for me to keep this solid form? You mortals are so limited, having to drag around your bits of bone and flesh."

"You tried to drown me!" I shout in her smug face.

"No! I just wanted us to be friends forever. Can you blame me?"

"Sure I blame you. You played on my sympathy because you knew I was a softie. You used me!"

"As much as you used me, Hannah," she says quietly.

229

I think about this for a moment. Spending time with Cady did fill the hole that Sara and Luisa left in my life when they went away for the summer. Cady made my days exciting, and knowing her made me do things I never would have dared before. But she did try to kill me. "Friendship is about trust, not about pulling a *friend's* head underwater. You don't get it, do you?"

"I get it," she says in the weariest of voices. You'd think *she'd* been the one who almost drowned. She sits down across from me, her legs scissored under her, her arms hugging herself as if to keep her body inside its walls. "You came because you wanted to, Hannah."

"No, you made me do it!"

She shakes her head. "I couldn't have, unless, in your heart of hearts, you really wanted to come swimming in Moonlight Lake."

"Not true!" Even as I shout it, I know she's right.

"Are you going to be mad forever?" Cady asks.

"Depends. I want to know what happened that night on the balcony."

"The balcony. Why do you care about that?" she blurts. "Ask me something that isn't so boring."

I take a deep breath. "Okay, why did you go to live with Vivienne and Anthony?"

"And their three bratty monsters? That's what they were, spoiled little beasts in that big, fancy mansion."

"Are Scooter and I spoiled beasts because we live in Nightshade? If you could see how much work it needs . . . Doesn't matter what you think about us. Tell me why you lived in Nightshade."

"If you want to know, you'll have to come with me into my memory."

It sounds a lot like, *Come swim in Moonlight Lake at midnight,* which makes me jittery. I shouldn't go. Mom and Dad would be so furious. But if they find out I snuck back into the forest, they'll be angry anyway, and I'll deserve whatever they dish out to me. I'll be grounded with no phone for the rest of my natural life. But it's worth it, so I tuck my hair behind my ears and go with Cady because, she's right, I want to.

She tells me to close my eyes, and when I open them I'm in Boston, Massachusetts, in 1898, on the day after Thanksgiving. The subway's just been completed. I'm at the Scollay Square station with the huge clock. Roman numerals. It's twenty after four, nearly dark.

"I'm eleven years old," Cady says. "Small for my age. My parents, heartless souls that they are, leave me with a zoo-keeper, Nanny Bridget, who might as well be a lion tamer for all the tenderness she offers. Do you see her with her huge feet and her face the color of corned beef?"

"Clearly."

"I wave good-bye to my mother and father at the sub-way station and trudge home with the nanny, who limps on those platypus feet. I'm furious, but I refuse to cry. My parents are on their way to the dock to board the SS *Portland*. At seven o'clock, Nanny Bridget tells me gleefully, their ship will leave port as it does every night, bound for Portland, Maine. They call her — the ship, not the nanny — the *Titanic* of New England. She's a side-wheeler paddle boat, great for river sailing, not the open seas."

"But safe," I assure us both. "Must be, if she sails every night."

"Unless there's a ferocious storm," Cady says, and all at once we're on the ship, and I feel the wind whipping at the woolen shawl clasped around my shoulders, over my coat. The wind bruises my cheeks and rips every pin out of my hair. My long coat lodges between my knees and nearly knocks me backward. We're being tossed from left to right, port to starboard. The SS *Portland*'s stern tips into the sea. Icy water soaks my coat, my dress, through my petticoats, clear to my underwear. I'm clutching the rail of the boat, watching shooting waves crash onto the wooden planks of the floor and seep through the cracks to the deck below. My stomach sours, threatening to pour its contents into the sea, and I close my eyes, preparing to be tossed overboard.

"Stop it!" I cry, and as suddenly as she began it, Cady calms the storm and we're back in the cemetery.

"A passing ship hears four short blasts. Do you know what that means? It's a nautical distress signal."

My head's still reeling, and I'm chilled to the bone. "What happens? What *happens*?" My stomach is beginning to settle and the icy chill is yielding to the sun — the very sun I'd griped about a few minutes ago for its heartless heat.

"The SS *Portland* and 190 people on board, all the crew and all the passengers, are swallowed by the sea. And that's how I end up at Aunt Vivienne and Uncle Anthony's house with their hellion children. You see? She was my mother, and she wasn't. She was my aunt by marriage because she was married to my uncle, but she was also my foster mother."

She lets that sink in. I guess *sink* isn't the best word, under the circumstances. Anyway, I'm not comfortable breaking the silence for the longest time until finally I ask, "How do I know you're telling me the truth?"

Cady is shocked. "Have I ever lied to you?"

"All the time! Especially when you called me to Moonlight Lake and promised I'd be safe. You are pure evil, Cadence Stanhope."

A look of such heartbreaking grief crosses her face. I've gone too far. She rises effortlessly. You could almost say she floats *ghost-like* away from me.

"I'm sorry I said that, Cady."

"All these girls," she says, panning her hand around the other six graves. "You think I lured each one to Moonlight Lake and drowned them. You do, admit it."

"Yes," I murmur.

"Hah!" Her laugh is frightening. It ricochets off all the trees around us and bounces back to her. "Here's the truth, Hannah. The truth. I invited them to Moonlight Lake at midnight. I would have given anything to have them come deep into the water and spend eternity with me. That's how desperately lonely I was. Am."

I gasp in horror as I'm shaken by the dreadful loneliness, the absolute *aloneness*, that Cadence Stanhope must feel, and it never goes away. I have friends. I have parents who love me and take care of me. I have sisters and brothers. I have a home, my own room, and teachers and coaches and good food and a brain that works (usually) and all five senses in good operating order. She has nothing. I'm drowning in her sorrow, and I see in her face how embarrassed she is to be sharing it with me.

And then, in a whispery voice that I have to strain to catch, she says, "I invited them all, and lots of others, to swim with me at midnight. But you . . . you are the only one who came."

CHAPTER FORTY-FIVE

I BLINK AWAY THE TEARS WELLING UP BEHIND MY eyelids. "And the other girls, the ones who didn't come to Moonlight Lake?"

"Gone, all of them. Well, they must be. So many of your years have passed. I guess their families buried them when their time came to move beyond this world. I have only their empty graves and names to keep me company."

"Such as Olivia Bainbridge?" I watch for her reaction, and she seems startled that I'd mention Olivia. "My sister knew her a little. She died in 2009, when she was thirteen. Did you have anything to do with that?"

"No. Thirteen doesn't interest me."

What a curious response, but I keep prodding her.

"So why is her grave here? Was she someone special? Maybe the best of all the girls?"

Cady's eyes jump around. "I never actually met Olivia."

"Then I don't get it."

Now her eyes zero in on me, as if she's wondering how much she can trust me. "You really want to know?" She sounds irritated, but softens a little. "It was right after Olivia passed. Her mother came to the forest with a heart as heavy as stone. She wandered for hours and accidentally found my little graveyard. I talked to her. I suppose because she was so sad, she didn't seem freaked out. Lots of people who come here are, you know."

I do, but I don't say anything, because Cady needs to talk.

"I think she knew that I was from the world beyond, the one Olivia was in. She asked me if I would keep Olivia remembered here among the other girls. How could I say no to a mother who loved her daughter so much?"

Unlike Cady's own mother. "Did Olivia . . . did her spirit come to you?"

"Once I sensed she was nearby, but she quickly drifted away from me." Cady twirls her hand in the air to show she means far, far away. "So now you know why I have her grave here. She came the closest to me."

Again, her look of grief and loneliness breaks my heart. "Sit down, please," I say quietly. "Tell me what happened on the balcony."

She sits beside me; I slide over so we can share her gravestone, making sure our shoulders don't touch.

Her voice is hollow and distant, and that reminds me about the orange yarn in the cabin: tangled time, raveling and unraveling. "Vivienne hates me. She thinks I pushed her over the wall, and that's why she died."

"Did you?" I ask, holding my breath.

"No."

"I'm so glad. I needed to hear you say that, Cady, because here's a news flash for you. She thinks she pushed *you* over the wall when she reached out to touch your face."

"How do you know what she thinks?"

Should I tell her? I take the plunge. "She's at Nightshade. I've seen her, or at least she's made herself known to Scooter and me, even to Gracie."

"I had no idea." Cady sinks into herself the way a cake sags in the middle — all still there, just compressed.

"Vivienne blames herself. She believes that she reached for you, and you jerked away from her hand and tumbled backward."

"That's not how it happened at all!" Cady cries. "I couldn't stand people touching me, especially her, with her dull, lifeless eyes trying to see me with her fingers. Out there on that balcony, we were both in the dark, but I could see by moonlight; she couldn't. I pushed her hand away, harder than I needed to, and *she* lost her balance. I reached out to grab her to keep her from cascading over the wall. Our hands clasped and . . . and . . . I don't know what happened after that, except we were both flying until we came to rest in a soft bed of warm water."

Is *that* what dying is like? No! I'd fiercely fight for my life, like I did in the lake. "Cady, listen to me. It wasn't your fault."

"It was! It was!"

"And it wasn't Vivienne's fault, either. My dad's carpenter told me about the slapdash job the builders did when they added on that balcony. The floor gave way, and the wall came crashing down, and you both plummeted into the pool. It wasn't anybody's fault but the carpenters'."

I take her hand, which she starts to pull away, then lets it rest in mine, as soft as duck down. "All these years, eons," she begins, "you can't imagine the huge guilt that's eaten away at me for sending Vivienne to her death."

"But you didn't!" I repeat.

"I didn't? I *didn't*!" Cady pulls me to my feet and dances me around wildly. We bump into trees, sending birds flying from tree to tree. She lets go of me and leaps over a tree stump, then chins herself and swings on a limb that's fragile enough to snap off if I put even a tiny bit of weight on it. We drop back to the soft ground cover.

"How many times have you heard me say I'm a free spirit, Hannah?"

"Lots of times, whenever it was convenient."

"I lied."

"You? I can't believe it."

"Now, after a hundred and twenty of your years, I *am* free, finally. Thank you!" Her eyes narrow. "It's going to take some time to get used to this," she says, brightening again. "But I've got lots of time!"

"So now you and Vivienne have to forgive each other. I don't know how ghosts work things out," I say with a sharp laugh, "but I'm beginning to understand how the living do. You've got to come to Nightshade and talk to Vivienne. Well, maybe *talk* isn't the right word. You know what I mean."

"Yes," she says, the eyes that used to drill into me shining now. They're the shade Scooter described about my iPad — sparkly silvery-blue, like water in sunlight. Belladonna eyes.

"You have to forgive each other, Cady, because Vivienne is a lonely, restless soul, just like you. And she's blind; she needs a guide."

"I'll do my best, but you've noticed that my best isn't always great. The cameo, it was hers, you know, but she didn't give it to me. I dug around in her jewelry box and found it under a bunch of other stuff the night . . . well, the night of the balcony. I thought, since she was blind, she'd never notice it missing."

I reach into my pocket and pull out the cameo. "Do the right thing, Cady, even if it feels wrong."

She reaches for it and holds it in both wavery hands. "I'll give it back to Vivienne. That's the first thing I'll do."

"Good start. Now, let's make a deal. Come to Nightshade. You and Vivienne get straightened out with each other so you can stop telling lies and saying mean things and burning down perfectly rotten cabins and trying to —" At this point my heart skips a few beats — "Stop trying to drown friends. Promise?"

She nods, and I try with all my heart to believe her. "And Vivienne needs to stop snatching pearls away from me and breaking tea cups and lightbulbs. Did you catch that, Vivienne?" I shout to the treetops.

There's no response, but I don't expect one from her in Cady's territory.

"What will you do on your end of the deal, Hannah?"

Good question. What kind of promises do you make to a living, breathing dead person? I give it serious thought while Cady fidgets and drums her fingers on the grass.

"My parents are going to be so mad that I slipped out of the house against their orders, and they'll probably ground me until I'm seventy. But whenever they get over it, I promise I'll come here to visit you. Absolutely no swimming, though. Wading, maybe. And no making people do things they don't want to do."

"You wanted to swim in Moonlight Lake," Cady reminds me.

I refuse to admit that. "Keep in mind it won't be as easy for me to come here in the winter or on stormy days. I'm not trudging through snow, and I don't want to be leaning on a tree that's struck by lightning in the middle of a storm."

"Mortals," Cady scoffs. "Afraid of everything."

She is so irritating, even now!

"I wish I hadn't said that stuff about you and your sister when she leaves home. Or about Scooter being a faker and a pest."

That's the closest someone like Cady comes to saying *I'm sorry*. "I forgive you for the things you said." Long pause, then, "I'm not sure I'm ready to forgive you for trying to drown me."

"I would have rescued you at the last minute," she says, but I'm not convinced it's true.

CHAPTER FORTY-SIX

THE SUN IS CREEPING HIGHER IN THE SKY, AND I'M squinting in the intense rays. I could turn my back to the sun, but I don't want to move, don't want to interfere with our conversation.

"You're a really nice girl, Hannah," Cady says. "I *would* have rescued you at the last minute. That's the truth. Believe me, because I'm way out of practice being nice. I was probably a decent kid the first year or two of my life."

"Until Nanny Bridget the Lion Tamer trained you. Oh, and I guess it's a long shot, but I have to ask. Did you know my great-grandparents a long time ago?"

"Just because I've lived forever doesn't mean I've known everybody on earth."

"You've known everybody who ever lived in Nightshade. You seem to know everything that goes on there. You slip in and out of the house quickly. What do you do, slide under the door? Walk through walls?"

Cady laughs — that body-shaking laugh is what I like

best about her. "We don't slither under doors or walk through walls, not when an open door is so much easier."

"However you did it, you took my nail polish and my music box and moved the cameo from my closet shelf. I know why you did those things."

"Why is that?" she asks sharply, and yeah, she's still got that sharp edge to her, but I can give her a dose of her own medicine.

"Scooter says even a cockroach wants to be noticed."

"That's insulting!"

"That's why Vivienne does the mischievous things she does — just so we know she's there. And by the way, you owe me a music box."

She sings, "Georgia named her, Georgia claimed her, Sweet Georgia Brown!"

"So about my great-grandparents," I try again. "It would have been around 1946, so they were pretty young. My Nana Fiona was just a baby. Cecil and Moira Flynn, does that ring a bell?"

Her eyes are focused far away. "I sort of remember a baby toddling around the Nightshade yard. Her mother, was that Moira? I remember her because she was the one who did all the wood chopping. The woman could really handle an axe."

"Yes, that sounds like my great-grandmother!"

"She came outside and found her baby playing with me and asked who I was. I panicked and vanished right before her eyes."

"That's what you're famous for. So maybe you're part of the reason why Cecil and Moira only lived in the house for a year. Between Vivienne's doings and you, they thought the house was cursed."

"Isn't it?" Cady's chuckle is sinister. She *is* a ghost, after all. "You'll get older, and I won't. When you're eighteen, and I'm still a nasty-tempered child, you'll think I'm deadly boring."

"You'll never be boring!" We both shake with laughter, and it's a tremendous release of all the feelings that have been piling up like a load of bricks on my shoulders. I can start to shrug them off.

With a big goofy smile, Cady says, "I can't promise that I won't get snarky from time to time. I have a long history of snarkiness."

"Me too, though mine isn't as long as yours. I'm only twelve."

"I'm always twelve. Remember, sometimes I won't look like this, with skin and meat on my bones and this beautiful hair." She tries to tuck it behind her ears, the way I do, but her helmet-hair won't stay tucked. "It's sure hard doing this whole-body thing. Think of it this way. It's as if you've been riding your bike up a mountain for thirty minutes, and when you get to the crest, you collapse. I'm close to that point." She shudders and wavers, a sail in the wind. "Whatever you're going to say, better say it fast."

I look at her, so tired and so hopeful. "Here's my promise, Cady. I will always come back to see you, even if I can't *see* you. Kind of the way Vivienne will see you. Sometimes I'll bring Scooter. Oh, and Luisa and Sara."

She wrinkles her nose. "Scooter, yeah. Those others, not too often. I'd like to meet Nana Fiona, though."

Cady's hand in mine begins to fade away, like a shadow when the sun slides behind a mountain. Suddenly, she's gone, and her absence carves a chunk right out of my heart, because it's deep-down lonely among these graves.

A warm comfort streams through my mind, a wave of light and thought. Is that Cady, lingering with me? I hope so, because it's something that I can roll around in my imagination and knead like Nana Fiona's bread dough into a beautiful shape, and I believe it's the thought that Cady wants me to tuck away in my heart and mind forever:

I always knew you were an honest and true friend.

ABOUT THE AUTHOR

Lois Ruby is the author of several books for middle graders and teens, including *The Doll Graveyard, Rebel Spirits, Steal Away Home, The Secret of Laurel Oaks,* and *Strike! Mother Jones and the Colorado Coal Field War.* She and her husband live in Albuquerque, New Mexico, at the foothills of the awesome Sandia Mountains. While traveling, Lois explores ghostly locations in Kansas, Pennsylvania, New Mexico, and even a few spots in Australia, Spain, and Thailand. No spirits have tapped her on the shoulder yet, but she's ready for that to happen any time now. Please visit Lois at www.loisruby.com.

HAUNTINGS

A spine-tingling scare in every story...

READ THEM ALL!

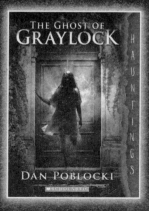

YOU'RE IN FOR THE FRIGHT OF YOUR LIFE!

Catch the
MOST WANTED
Goosebumps® villains
UNDEAD OR ALIVE!

SPECIAL EDITIONS

■SCHOLASTIC

scholastic.com/goosebumps

GBMW42

What's on your  list?

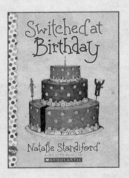